Jaspreet Singh was born in Punjab, and brought up in Kashmir and in several cities in India. He is a former research scientist with a PhD in chemical engineering from McGill University, Montreal. His debut short-story collection, *Seventeen Tomatoes*, won the 2004 McAuslan First Book Prize. *Chef*, his first novel, won the Georges Bugnet Award for Fiction and was shortlisted for four awards including the 2009 Commonwealth Writers' Prize for Best Book in the Region. It was also longlisted for the 2010 International IMPAC Dublin Literary Award. He lives in the Canadian Rockies.

CHEF

Kip Singh is timorous and barely twenty when he arrives for the first time at General Kumar's camp, nestled in the shadow of the mighty Siachen Glacier that claimed his father's life. He is placed under the supervision of Chef Kishen, a fiery, anarchic mentor who guides Kip towards the heady spheres of food and women. As a Sikh, Kip feels secure in his allegiance to India, the right side of this interminable conflict. Until, one oppressively close day, a Pakistani 'terrorist' with long, flowing hair is swept up on the banks of the river and changes everything.

JASPREET SINGH

CHEF

Complete and Unabridged

ULVERSCROFT
Leicester

First published in Great Britain in 2010 by
Bloomsbury Publishing
London

First Large Print Edition
published 2010
by arrangement with
Bloomsbury Publishing
London

British Library CIP Data

Singh, Jaspreet, *1969* –
Chef.
1. Cooks- -Fiction. 2. Jammu and Kashmir (India)
- -Fiction. 3. Large type books.
I. Title
813.6–dc22

ISBN 978–1–44480–448–5

Published by
F. A. Thorpe (Publishing)
Anstey, Leicestershire

Set by Words & Graphics Ltd.
Anstey, Leicestershire
Printed and bound in Great Britain by
T. J. International Ltd., Padstow, Cornwall

This book is printed on acid-free paper

They make a desolation and call it peace.

Galgacus, 84 AD

The cold is eating into the center of my brain.

Thomas Bernhard

One

1

For a long time now I have stayed away from certain people.

I was late getting to the station and almost missed the *Express* because of the American President. His motorcade was passing the Red Fort, not far from the railway terminal. The President is visiting India to sign the nuclear deal. He is staying at the Hotel Taj and the chefs at the hotel have invented a new kebab in his honor. All this in today's paper. Rarely does one see the photo of a kebab on the front page. It made my mouth water.

Not far from me, a little girl is sitting on the aisle seat. A peach glows in her hand. Moments ago she asked her mother, What do we miss the most when we die? And I almost responded. But her mother put a thick finger on her lips: Shh, children should not talk about death, and she looked at me for a brief second, apologetically. Food, I almost said to the girl. We miss peaches, strawberries, delicacies like Sandhurst curry, kebab pasanda and rogan josh. The dead do not eat marzipan. The smell of bakeries torments them day and night.

3

Something about this exchange between mother and daughter has upset me. I look out the window. The train is cutting through villages. I don't even know their names. But the swaying yellow mustard fields and the growing darkness fills me with disquiet about the time I resigned from the army. I find myself asking the same question over and over again. Why did I allow my life to take a wrong turn?

Fourteen years ago I used to work as chef at the General's residence in Kashmir. I remember the fruit orchard by the kitchen window. For five straight years I cooked for him in that kitchen, then suddenly handed in my resignation and moved to Delhi. I never married. I cook for my mother. Now after a span of fourteen years I am returning to Kashmir.

It is not that in all these years I was not tempted to return. The temptation was at times intense, especially when I heard about the quake and the rubble it left behind. But the earth shook mostly on the *enemy* side. During my five years of service I was confined to the Indian side — the more beautiful side.

The beauty is still embedded in my brain. It is the kind that cannot be shared with others. Most important things in our lives, like recipes, cannot be shared. They remain within us with a dash of this and a whiff of that and trouble our bones.

★ ★ ★

The tumor is in your brain, said the specialist. (Last week exactly at three o'clock my CAT scan results came back to the clinic. The dark scan looked quite something inside that box of bright light.) His finger pointed towards an area which resembled a patch of snow, and next to it was a horrifying shape like the dark rings of a tree. Three months to a year maximum, he said. Suddenly I felt very weak and dizzy. My voice disintegrated. The world around me started withering.

I walked the crowded street back home. Cutting through my own cloud, stepping through the fog. My mother greeted me at the door. She knew. My mother already knew. She (who cooked every meal for me when I was young) knew what I did not know myself. She handed me a letter, and slowly walked to her bed.

The letter was postmarked Kashmir. After fourteen years General Sahib finally mailed the letter, and that thin piece of paper delighted me and brought tears to my eyes. His daughter is getting married. In hurriedly scribbled lines he requested me to be the chef for the wedding banquet.

I read the letter a second time, sitting at the kitchen table. My answer was obviously going to be a no. I was not even planning to respond. I felt dizzy. But in the evening while preparing soup I changed my mind. I make all big decisions while cooking. Mother is bedridden most of the time and I served as usual in her room at eight in the evening. I did not reveal the trouble brewing in my brain. During dinner I simply read her the General's letter.

'Are you sure?' she asked. 'You want to go?'

'Of course,' I said. 'It is impossible to say no.'

Dear Kip, Several times in the past I thought of writing to you, but I did not. You know me well, my whole life in the army has been geared to eliminate what is from a practical stand point non-essential.

My daughter (whom you last saw as a child) is getting married, and she is the one who forced me to write this letter. I have heard that your mother is sick, but this is a very important event in our life, and we would like you to be the chef at the wedding. I do not want some new duffer to spoil it.

You are the man for this emergency. I want to see you and I am tired and have much to talk over and plan with you. This wedding feast is perhaps my last battle and I would like for us to win it. I am sure you will not disappoint me.

Yours affectionately,

Lt. General Ashwini Kumar (Retired), VrC, AVSM, PVSM.

Former GOC-in-C, Northern Command.

The General's daughter used to call me 'Kip-Ing' (instead of Kirpal Singh). Since then 'Kip' has stuck. In the army everyone has a second name. General Sahib's nickname was 'Red', but it was rarely mentioned in his presence.

'How many days will you spend there?' Mother asked.

'Seven,' I said. 'Seven or eight days. I must go, Mother. The neighbor will take care of you. Eating someone else's food will do you good.'

Mother did not finish the dal soup. Her frail head rested on two white pillows and she held my arm as if we were not going to see each other again.

I urged her to take the yellow tablets and capsules. She agreed only after I raised my voice. I rarely raise my voice in the presence of Mother. Something inside me was definitely changing.

It was then I showed her the wedding card:

Rubiya Kumar
weds
Shahid Lone

'So the General's daughter has decided to marry a Muslim?' she asked.

'Not just a Muslim,' I added, 'but one from the other side of the border.'

Let me put this straight. Sahib is not prejudiced against the Muslims. There were Muslim soldiers in our regiment, and he never once discriminated against any of them to my knowledge. But, of course, General Sahib is not pleased with the wedding. I have read the letter twice, and I sense his hands must have been shaking when he held the pen. Sahib gave his youth to our nation to keep the Pakistanis away, he fought two wars, and now his own daughter is marrying one of them. Did so many soldiers lose their lives for one big nothing?

This train is moving slower than a mountain mule. The engine is old, I know. It resembles me in many ways. But the railway-wallahs insist on calling it an *Express*.

I readjust my glasses, and my gaze drifts from one fuzzy face to another. They will last longer than me — the ears and eyes and noses of other people. Faint scent of pickles fills the compartment. Loud and hazy conversations. Flies have started hovering over the little girl's peach.

Once I prepare the perfect wedding banquet, General Sahib will refer me to top specialists in the military hospital, and they will start treatment right away. I have a high regard for military doctors. For my mother's sake, I must live a little longer. I don't know why I raised my voice in her presence. She needs me more than ever. I must live a little bit longer.

Perhaps it was simply the selfish wish *to live just a little bit longer* that made me change my mind.

But things must sort out first. Before I begin work for the wedding I want the General to sort out things between us. For the last fourteen years every day I expected a letter from him. And now the wait is over, the letter is in my pocket. I had expected the letter to be heavy, to carry the entire weight of our past, but he offered me nothing. No explanation. I want him to sort out things between us. Not pretend as if there had been a simple misunderstanding.

I still remember the day I had arrived in Kashmir the first time. The mountains and lakes were covered with thick fog. I was nineteen. And I had bought a second-class ticket on this very train. For some reason I remember the train moved faster then.

2

I must have fallen asleep. I am woken up by a tap on my shoulder. 'Is this bag yours, is this one yours?' Two police-wallahs in our compartment. 'Yes, that one is mine,' says the civilian man occupying the aisle seat, the girl no longer there. One police-wallah sticks labels on already identified luggage. 'And the brown suitcase on the rack belongs to my missus,' the man says.

'Whose is this big trunk?'

'Mine,' I say.

'You don't look like a commissioned officer.'

'It used to belong to a general.'

'Show me your ID card.'

'I forgot my card.'

'What is the name of the general?'

'He is retired now.'

'Name?'

'He is the new Governor of Kashmir.'

'Name?'

'General Kumar.'

The police-wallahs look at me with contempt. They have rifles slung around their necks. The younger one turns on his flashlight.

'What *things* are there inside?'

I do not respond. I take pity on their contemptible tasks.

'Open it.'

One of them transfers the heavy trunk to the aisle, and I hand him the key. He is rough-handling the bottles, and he does not read the labels. His face resembles the face of people who don't take responsibility for their actions.

'What is all this?'

'Don't you see?' The middle-aged woman sitting close by comes to my rescue. 'This is heeng and that one is cinnamon . . . cardamom, coriander, cloves, fenugreek, crushed pomegranate, poppy seeds, rose petals, curry leaves, nutmeg and mace.'

'Why so many spices?' asks the first police-wallah.

'Are you a woman?' asks the second.

Chuckles from the two of them. 'Carrying an entire kitchen on the train?'

'The only reason we will let you go is because your trunk is not a real coffin,' one of them says from the other end of the bogie, making eye contact with me, staring.

They chuckle louder after making that odd remark, and leave.

Then silence. Only the sound of the train.

Outside I see India passing by. I readjust my glasses. It is raining mildly, and I am glad it is raining because India looks beautiful in the rain. Rain hides the melancholy of this land, ugliness as well. Rain helps me forget my own self. I see a face reflected in the window. Who is that man with spots of gray in his hair? What have I become? But certain things never change. I have the face of someone who is always planning serious work, someone who does not know how to take time off. Now even that will be snatched away from me.

None of my fellow passengers understood the police-wallahs when they said, 'The only reason we have let you go is because your trunk is not a real coffin.' Our country is a country with a short memory. They don't remember the coffin scam which took place in the army during the war with Pakistan and cost the General his promotion. Because of the scam he could not become the chief of army staff. He was innocent really. Officers below him, jealous of Sahib's abilities, screwed him. Sahib did not get the respect he deserved. There is no way I am going to explain to the civilians the coffin scam. Even if I tried they would not understand.

The middle-aged woman is surveying me, looking at me from the corners of her eyes. She is eager to ask me thousands of questions. Her face resembles a plate of samosas left overnight in rain. The man sitting across the aisle just said he is proud of the Indian army. After the police-wallahs left, he asked me, 'What did you do in the army, sir?'

'I kept the top brass healthy and cheerful.'

'What is it exactly you did, sir?'

'I was the General's chef for five years.'

'Oh, you were a cook,' he said and controlled his smile. His wife could not control herself. She looked up from the glossy magazine, laughed. The middle-aged woman could not control her laughter either. Civilians.

Then suddenly as if to break silence, he asked: 'Have you ever won a woman's heart with your cooking, sir?'

I did not reply.

'But you must have?'

'There are no women in the army,' I said.

'But sir. Women fall for men in the army. You, sir, had the biggest weapon in your hand. Cooking. Did you ever make someone fall in love, sir?'

'Sorry,' I said. 'I am looking for a chai-wallah. Did you hear a vendor selling tea?'

'Oh, we have tea in our thermos. Please pour some for sir.'

'No, no, thank you very much.'

I turned to the window and the conversation stopped. The view outside the window was far more interesting.

3

India is passing through the night. Night, just like rain, hides the ugliness of a place so well. We are running behind the backs of houses. Thousands of tiny lights have been turned on inside them. Towns pass by, and villages. I remember my first journey to Kashmir on this train. It was a very hot day, and despite that, passengers were drinking tea, and the whole compartment smelled of a wedding. Girls in beautiful saris and salwar-kameezes sat not far from me; some of them spoke hardly any English. Their skins had the shine of ripe fruits. How shy I was then. How much I yearned to talk to them, but I pretended that I was not interested. I had picked up the paper the man in the corner seat had discarded, and hid my face behind the news. I would stealthily peek at the girls and when one or two returned my gaze I would hide once again behind words. One time my eyes locked with the eyes of an oval-faced girl, and this created an awkward moment. She started whispering, and then suddenly an exclamation was followed by loud laughter, and I felt they were all laughing at me, and I hid again behind the paper. How I yearned to talk to them, and how I desired for them to leave me alone in the carriage because I could not endure so many of them, and I wanted them to carry on with their usual business without bothering me, and when they disembarked at a strange platform how alone I had felt in that near-empty carriage. I had missed my chance. A beautiful opportunity had presented itself, but I had spoiled it. Partly to deal with loneliness and partly to deal with the absence of girls I began reading the paper. Several times I read the article which had shielded me from the beauties. It was accompanied by a large photograph of the body of a soldier.

BODY OF A SOLDIER FOUND
AFTER 53 YEARS

Trekkers on a remote stretch of Hima-layan glacier have found the fully preserved body of a soldier 53 years after he died in a plane crash. They discovered the corpse, still in an overcoat uniform, with personal documents in the pockets. The discovery was reported yesterday at the base camp. The team also found aircraft parts close to the soldier, suggesting there could be other bodies buried in ice.

It is believed the crash occurred in early 1934. The soldier may have been flying to or from Ladakh, the high altitude area in Kashmir.

In 1934 India had yet to be partitioned by the British to become 'India' and 'Pakistan'. So it is not clear whether the body belongs to India or Pakistan. The two countries have fought four wars, three of them over Kashmir.

Kashmir. It was my first time, and I found the place different from the way Delhi-wallahs describe it, as paradise, or shadow of paradise. I was a young man, but old enough to separate romance from reality. There was thick fog and it was very cold. I did not have a proper jacket. I had arrived with only one suitcase and the recruitment letter in my pocket. By the time I stood on the lawns of the General's residence the sound of the train had simply disappeared from my mind. A uniformed man accompanied me from the gate-posts to Sahib's residence, the Command House, located on a hill overlooking the golf course. I must have waited for half an hour on the lawns. I thought I was going to die of cold when a middle-aged man stepped out of the house. He was wearing an apron. The hair on his head was closely cropped. His face, clean-shaven with thin eyebrows, ears unusually long. The man's body had a

17

muscular appeal to it. A black dog trotted ahead of him. The dog came to sniff me. I touched its muzzle.

'How old is he?' I asked.

'We are all growing old,' the man said. 'Fourteen, maybe, the dog is fourteen.'

'How long do dogs live, sir?'

He did not answer, but took off slowly in the wind towards a patch of vegetable garden, fencing around it. He opened a little wooden gate and shut it. The dog circumambulated the fence while on the other side the man stooped and plucked leaves of what to me looked like fenugreek or coriander. How the vegetables grew in the extreme cold was beyond my imagination.

'Come.' He asked me to follow him.

I handed him the recruitment paper.

'Not now,' he said.

On the way to the kitchen the man patted me on my back. He was an inch or two taller than me. Something about that pat made me feel uncomfortable.

'Follow me,' he said. 'The General's ADC has told me about you. He has given me the instructions.'

'What do I call you, sir?'

'I am Chef.'

'Sir.'

'Call me Chef Kishen.'

'Sir.'

'Just call me Chef.'

'Yessir.'

'Follow me with your luggage,' he said.

We entered his room, which was between the kitchen and the servants' quarters. The place reeked of shaving cream; cuttings from Hindi newspapers covered the walls: photos of Bombay actresses in revealing saris, including my favorite, Waheeda. On the side table a tape recorder was playing music unfamiliar to my ears. German music, he said. I wouldn't have imagined, I said. *Does this bother you?* No sir. Top mewjik, he said. There were two beds side by side, and they formed a huge shadow on the floor. The square shadow on the wall came from the tape recorder. Chef pointed towards the smaller bed. Suddenly my body felt the exhaustion of a long journey. I dumped my suitcase and sat down on the bed.

'Not now,' he said. 'Keep following.'

The kitchen. Scent of cumin, ajwain and cardamom. On the table, a little pile of nutmeg. Thick, oily vapor rose from the pot on the stove. The room was warm and spacious, the window high and wide. Tiny drops of condensation covered the top of the glass. Smoke soared towards the ceiling in shafts of light. I noticed many shiny pots and pans hanging on the whitewashed walls. And strings of lal mirchi, and idli makers, and thalis, and conical molds for kulfi. In the corner the tandoor was ready. Its orange glow stirred in the utensils on the walls. I walked to the oven and stooped over. A wave of heat hit my cheeks. It was then he put his arm around my shoulder and took me towards the dining room. He said, 'Kitchen without a memsahib is a nice place to work in.'

'Sir.'

'See that woman looking down at us?'

'Sir.'

'She was the memsahib.'

The painting was seven or eight feet tall, and so was the beautiful woman. Her eyes were big and wide open. Her brows, fearless. Skin, the color of cinnamon. She was wrapped in a graceful red sari.

'Sahib used to love her as if she were a Mughal queen and she in turn loved him the way she loved her dog.'

'Sir.'

'She loved me too.'

'Yes, sir.'

'What do you mean *yes, sir*? She was a bitch. Memsahibs is people that controls the kitchen. She counted spoons. She counted to test the reliability of staff. That woman banned cooking without a shirt on, and I had to wear at least a banian in her presence. Aprons appeared suddenly. She cooked the dessert herself on Tuesdays and made me taste it and one wrong (but honest) word would make that woman swear in English. It was hard for me. The hardest thing to do is to hold my tongue, Kirpal.'

'Sir.'

'That woman refused to change recipes. To disturb a recipe is to disturb the soul of the dead, she would say.'

Right then I heard loud voices coming towards the kitchen from other rooms. The bell rang for service. Chef replaced the server out on a cigarette break and dashed into Sahib's room with the tray of tea and samosas. The samosas smelled of pork. Sahib is fond of pork, he said before leaving the kitchen. There was rhythm in his legs. In Sahib's room I will also take *ardor* for dinner. He pronounced 'order' as *ardor*. It was one of the few English words in his vocabulary.

I soon learned about him. Chef had joined the army as an ordinary soldier, and after an injury in the war he was sent to the Officers' Mess. During a meeting of the middle brass of the regiment he had committed his first error. He had refused to serve tea to a Muslim officer.

'I refused tea to that man,' said Chef. 'The

problem with *those people* is that they smell. *Badboo*. That is why. The colonel showed me his teeth and reprimanded me severely. I was transferred to the kitchen as a dishwasher, but within a few months I bounced back. I made the kitchen my territory and impressed the officers with my *above average* culinary abilities. The brigadier of the regiment chose me for a four-month training course in international cuisine conducted by the foreign embassies in Delhi. German, French, Chinese, Italian, Szechuan noodles, linguine with clam sauce, lamb provençal, Pavlova — that kind of food. You see, if I had not refused to serve tea to the Muslim officer I would never have become a chef. Understand?'

'Yes, sir,' I said.

4

It is almost midnight. The train picked up speed close to Panipat Station. The light in the ceiling is flickering. A miniature fan swivels and hurls hot air. Not a single thought I have is peaceful. The screeching sound of metal against metal competes with passengers pushing and jostling even at this insane hour. A child lowers the window, raises it again. Her parents are stirring in their sleep, mouths half open. Their faces move left to right and right to left as if to a pendulum. Diagonally across from me a honeymooning couple is sitting underneath brightly colored bags. The wife is young and pretty. (A white jasmine tucked in her hair.) I like the nape of her neck, and henna on hands. Her husband, in brown corduroy, is glued to the World Cup cricket commentary. It must be day in Australia. He is holding the transistor radio close to his ear. Now and then he lifts his free hand and runs a finger through the brand-new wife's hair. Such displays of emotion were not possible in public when I was a young man.

She asks him to turn off the radio; he

smiles and raises the volume. The peasants sitting next to him applaud: they too would like to know the score. The child on my right yawns. She is no longer playing her window game. The cricket commentary is interrupted by commercials and the hourly news. The newscaster's voice is convent-educated. Some would say sexy.

She begins with late-night news about the American President.

The President stunned our nation today by visiting the Gandhi Peace Memorial. Despite this gesture many of our countrymen are demonstrating in front of the American embassy in Delhi. The people have taken offence to dogs. This is what happened: yesterday just before the President's visit the security-wallahs tested the site with sniffer dogs. The people feel that the dogs have desecrated the site. Some are also angry and shocked because the Prime Minister of our country was frisked by the American bodyguards (on Indian soil) before he was allowed to shake hands with the President, said the newscaster. Last night at the state banquet the President delivered a speech saying that America was definitely going to sign the nuclear deal with India, and his country was also going to allow the import of Indian mangoes. Now that is interesting, I say to myself.

The man's pretty wife is putting kohl around her eyes, surveying her face in a miniature mirror, the shape of a perfect oval.

News is over. Back to cricket. The man, listening again. Please lower the volume, I request. He contorts his face. Please, I beg you, I say again. It is past midnight. He bows, apologizes, and to my surprise turns off the radio and begins reading the paper. As far as the dogs are concerned I don't think we Indians should object at all. Gandhi loved animals. The dogs have done no harm to the father of the nation. If we are hell-bent on taking offence then we must take offence to the local thugs and criminals who deliver long speeches paying so-called homage at the Peace Memorial.

On the front page of the paper there is a picture of the American President eating a mango. He is eating the reddish-yellow fruit with a knife and a fork. I see it in the flickering light. The picture is making me increasingly uncomfortable. This is not the proper way to eat a mango, I say to myself. They are supposed to be eaten the way Father used to.

Father never used a knife to cut mangoes, he would suck them.

He would eat several at a sitting, one by one, all varieties, sandhoori, dusshairi, langra, choussa, alphonso. He loved good food. Good chutney. He was right-handed but held a chapatti in his left; he scooped up the chutney with a torn bit of chapatti. If curried lamb was served, he liked gravy more than the pieces. He ate kebabs without a piyaz. Even now I can see him clearly. Father is home on a two-day leave from his regiment, he is eating dinner with another man in uniform, also a Sikh, I call him uncle, they are talking about colonels and generals, and war and enemy, us versus them. I can see this although I am hiding under the table. And I can hear them. Uncle's foot taps my leg. I run to my room, from under the table. Father scolds me mildly for not doing my home-work. From behind the curtain I watch Father sucking on the fruits one by one. Uncle has stopped eating, he is telling Partition stories, but Father continues. Even now I can see him squeezing the pulp upwards. To this day I remember his hands. His fingers were those of a musician.

But.

There are things he will never know. He has no idea about the anger I carry around to this day. Deep inside — so many unresolved emotions. Perhaps my cancer is the conse-quence of the shame and guilt and anger that never found a passage out of my body. The most important things in our lives can't be squeezed out.

I never wanted to join the army. In Delhi my desires were different. I had just had my eighteenth birthday. I woke up late that morning. Frying mustard oil and aloo parathas stung my eyes. Mother scolded me (from the kitchen) to hurry up. I rushed to the bathroom with soap and when I opened the door I saw my cousin was inside. I had opened the door thinking the bathroom was empty, but she was inside, washing herself. She was very beautiful, my cousin, a married woman, and later that day, at college, I could not forget her dark nipples. Drops of water moving, crawling on her cinnamon skin and wheat-colored breasts. I felt some strange forbidden joy. But at the same time I felt guilty, as if I had committed a crime. She was the first woman I had seen completely naked, and those two seconds kept coming back to me that day in the college, first during math class, and then during history. I saw her wet body everywhere in the classroom and I kept returning again and again to the moment she had buried her head in her hands (after a very brief eye contact) and I felt I could not live without touching her bare breasts. What was I doing in the classroom? The teacher was covering the subaltern history of Indians (especially Sikhs) who had died in Europe fighting the two World Wars. Outside it was very bright and hot. Through the window I noticed my mother rushing towards the college, accompanied by a man in a camouflaged uniform. I thought that my cousin had reported me, and I was to be punished.

Mother stood by the door and had a fast talk with the teacher, and right away the teacher instructed me in a soft voice to pack my books. Her face froze as I marched my shadow to the door. There was pin-drop silence in our class. It was then I sensed something terribly wrong had happened. The man standing behind Mother looked very stiff; his face had no spark and his uniform was crisp and starched without a wrinkle. He was holding a black cap in his hand.

They walked me close to the road beyond the spot where stray dogs were barking, a goods train passed by, parallel to the road, and the man asked if he could have a word with me.

'Young man, the whole nation is very proud of Major Iqbal Singh.'

There was a mist in Mother's eyes. Unlike other women she rarely wept in public. She held my hand and slowly quickened her step. We walked in the same direction. *Home.* That was the last time we walked together. The dogs didn't come after us.

Now that I think about it she too was fighting battles. While my father was fighting a war in Kashmir with the Pakistanis, my mother was fighting battles with herself. She stopped in the middle of the road and hugged me, then let me go. She wanted to be alone.

At home instead of Father and death, I kept thinking about my cousin's cinnamon body. That evening my cousin and her husband came along with many others to our house. They drank imported Coke and spouted the standard things. When the mourning was over I took the empty bottles into the street and lined them up and kicked them one by one, the bottles rolling further and further away from me. A plane passed overhead, creating a white cloud. The windows of our house rattled.

I knew then.

When I woke up the next morning stray dogs kept barking in the street, and my whole body felt sick. I felt his presence in the room. I see myself running up the stairs to the room where he kept his black military trunk. In the trunk I found his pistol and from the roof terrace I started aiming, shooting at the dogs in the street until mother screamed at me from the other side of the clothesline. People flocked to our house. What is wrong with you? Poor thing, I heard one say. You are the son of a very brave man. Why are you muddying your father's name? This boy has done nothing wrong, said Mother. She could speak no more. When the crowd left I heard the single bark of a dog on the pavement. It was the only one that did not flee like others towards the bazaar.

'How many did you kill?' asked Mother.

'None.'

'Don't lie to me.'

'One.'

'Dog killer.'

'One is injured,' I said.

Mother begged me not to join the army.

'You never wanted to.'

'I'm going to join Father's regiment.'

She begged me not to move to Kashmir. That place is foreign to us, it is filled with turmoil, she said. She tried to persuade me to follow my original plan: study two more years, get a civilian job and then get married.

'You're my only child,' she said.

I clicked my heels and saluted her, the way Father used to.

On the way to Kashmir the first time I took the train, I carried an old black and white photograph in my wallet. I recall saying to myself that the thing looked different now, because the man in the photo was actually dead. The officer's uniform, the medals on his chest, the epaulets, the turban with a red regimental ribbon, and the shining stars — everything looked different. Father is not alone in the photo, he is standing in the middle of the parade ground with three others. It is their graduation day. Father is the only one in a turban. With great amusement he is observing the caps of his fellow officers. The caps are floating in the air and are about to begin a sudden downward descent. (Cadets, the moment they become officers, follow an odd graduation ritual: they toss their caps up in the air to mark the turning point in their lives.) Father is unable to participate fully in the ritual. His turban is intact. He is one of them, but he is different. Like them he is young, filled with hope. Did he know then that soon he would become the yellow photograph in my hand? He could not have known then, and neither could I have known that soon his son would try to forget him, but the harder he would attempt, the more disastrously he would fail. On that train journey the photo terrified me. I remember opening the grimy window, tearing the thing into pieces, letting it go. There was thick fog outside, and the pieces went up and down in the wind and vanished in the fog. At the time a fellow passenger in the compartment was carrying a basket of unripe mangoes. Just like right now — this carriage has the same pungent odor.

5

When I think about my past, time begins flowing in a different way and my thoughts turn to the mountains of Kashmir, and to the river that begins at the toe of the glacier.

The river begins in India, crosses the border and flows into the enemy territory. In Pakistan time is half an hour behind India, and the moment the river crosses the border it moves backwards in time. But three or four mountains away it re-enters our side, becomes Indian again, and by doing so moves forward in time. This crossing of borders keeps happening over and over again.

General Sahib was the chief of Northern Command. He resided in the second biggest house in the capital city, Srinagar. From the slopes of the camp the river looked like a blue-skinned python flowing through the valley. There were nine bridges spanning the waters: the first was called *Zero*, and the second *Bridge Number One* and the last *Bridge Number Eight*. Not far from Zero Bridge was the old city with timber-framed houses and crowded bazaars and pagoda-shaped mosques. The most famous mosque was white, made entirely of marble, and it stood next to a green Sufi shrine. At the outskirts of the city were the ruins and the Mughal garden built by the Emperor in the seventeenth century. Our camp sat next to the garden on the slopes of a hill. Between the ruins and the camp was an eighteen-hole golf course and on its left was another hill with a white mansion on top. This was the Governor's residence, the Raj Bhavan, the biggest house in Srinagar. The Governor, I heard, loved international cuisine and once or twice (before my arrival) Sahib had loaned Chef Kishen to him.

General Sahib ate breakfast at six-thirty in the morning. Two days a week papaya and stuffed aloo-parathas (which he ate with his hands), and the rest of the time English breakfast of the Raj (with knife and fork). Lunch he ate in the office. We sent hot tiffin to his office building through the orderly.

The kitchen window faced the golf course, and I would watch Sahib play in the evenings with other officers, and on occasions with the Governor himself. Often I worried for them because we were so close to the land of the enemy. On the right side of the golf course, across the river, was a little village, and beyond the village, on the blue mountains, was the enemy. Often fighting would start on

34

the brown mountain, which belonged neither to us nor to them. The sound of machine guns would rebound in the valley and invade our lives. But then the guns would stop for a while and the delicious sounds of bugles and military bagpipes from our camp and the enemy camp would waft inside the kitchen, and mix with the sounds of coals in the tandoor.

Dinner was the main meal of the day. Sahib had good taste and appetite and a weakness for Kashmiri dishes. Mughlai mutton with turnips, rogan josh, kebab nargisi, lotus roots-n-rhizomes, gongloo, karam saag, the infinitely slow-cooked nahari, and the curd-flavored meatballs of gushtaba. He ate these dishes licking his fingers, and used knife and fork for foreign preparation only, for dishes from Italy, France, Spain, Greece and Russia.

Since Chef had received training at foreign embassies in Delhi, international cuisine was his greatest strength. But he taught me mostly to subvert those recipes. 'Foreigners have colonized us for a long time, Kip. Now it is our turn. We will take their food and make it our own . . .

'Pay attention to simple things, Kip. If one cannot deal with a simple dish properly, there is no way one will be able to handle the more sophisticated. Take a tomato, for instance.

What is the taste of this tomato? There is no such thing as the set *taste* of a tomato. Taste lies in the surface, the way you cut it . . .

'Before cutting a tomato, give it the reverence it deserves and ask: Tomato, what would you like to become? Do you want to be alone? Or do you prefer company? Apricot, what would you like to become? Would you like to become more than yourself in the company of saffron?

'Saffron, who are you?'

The kitchen opened onto a smaller room. In that room I would skin chickens, peel battalions of potatoes, slice chilies, and pluck coriander leaves off stems. Connected to this room was a larger room. There we ate or played cards and had meetings at the wooden table with Chef. Spitting was forbidden in this room.

Chef began work at six in the morning, and two days a week he would invite me in the evening to bike with him along the river. Calling Kashmir paradise does not do justice. The first PM of our country once said (in English): Kashmir is the face of a beloved that one sees in a dream and that fades away on awakening. Nehru knew Kashmir better than the leaders nowadays. Chef and I would bike past the Nehru Memorial, past the bakery on Residency Road, past Zero Bridge, past hundreds of houseboats with names like Neil Armstrong, Cleopatra, Texas Spitfire, Dawn of Paradise, Heevan, past the Dal Lake Floating Market, where vendors of fruits and vegetables sat in motionless shikaras, and the smell of fresh produce mingled with the odor of defecation, and we would make a loop and bike back to the Mughal garden, and it was there on the slopes of the garden one day he put his arm around my shoulder and pointed to the buildings in the valley below. State Assembly. Cricket Stadium. Post Office. Mughal Fort. Radio Kashmir. Governor's mansion. The city. It was a compact medieval city, punctuated by modern buildings and ancient ruins. Buddhist ruins. Hindu ruins. Muslim ruins. I was very moved by their presence.

'It is difficult to breathe here,' said Chef.

'Because of the ruins?' I asked.

'No, because there are so many mosques here. Understand?'

'No,' I said.

'You see that white marble building by the lake?'

'Yes, Chef.'

'Guess what?'

'Looks like a mosque. But it has only one minaret.'

'In that mosque some dangerous Kashmiris

37

meet to create trouble.'

'Trouble?'

'They talk about *azadi*. Freedom.'

'I see, Chef.'

'Lots of mosques down there.'

'The place looks like the city of mosques, Chef.'

'Fanatics!'

'Even inside our camp, Chef. On the left, I see that stone mosque.'

'No longer a mosque. The army converted it to good use. It is the military hospital, kid.'

The hospital windows (and the dome) were lit up orange by the last light. The sun was about to set.

'I am feeling cold, Chef.'

'There is a remedy,' he said.

'Remedy?'

'Get yourself a *phudee*.'

'A what, Chef?'

'A cavity.'

'What for?'

'Get yourself a woman.'

I shut my eyes. The wind whistled between the mountains.

'Chef, you should not say that.'

'Get yourself — '

'Chef, what does this city look like in winter?'

'A white calico,' he said. 'Snow covers all

the rooftops and streets down in the valley and hides all the ungainly parts, just like a sari hides the ungainly parts of a wom — '

'White, the color of mourning,' I stammered.

'Kip, no more mourning-forning,' he said.

'What is that?'

'You need a woman.'

'Chef, in summers are there mosquitoes in Kashmir?'

'Mosques and mosquitoes.'

'What?'

'The mosques we can manage, but we are still learning how to eradicate the mosquitoes.'

'How does one eradicate?'

'Hit them in the balls.'

'Chef is joking.'

'There is another way. If you make them fly out of the mosques, the wind will freeze their balls. You see the flags outside the mosques? Sometimes they flutter like insane creatures in the wind. Cold winds come from the glacier and madden them.'

'Where is the glacier?' I asked.

He pointed towards the distant mountains on my right, and my gaze remained fixed on the glaring whiteness that covered them.

'Siachen Glacier, kid.'

So that was Siachen. It was staring back at

us. I grew silent. I had been feeling its presence for a while. The beast had swallowed my father. Father's plane had crashed on Siachen. The wing landed not far from the bakery in Srinagar, but the main body of the plane disappeared in a deep crevasse.

'That glacier is bigger than the city of Bombay, kid.'

I took a deep breath.

'I knew your father,' he said, clearing his throat.

'Did you know him well?'

'Only from a distance. I knew him, he didn't know me. I was only a cook.'

I kept silent.

'Seeing the wing had fallen in the bazaar the loathsome Kashmiris stepped out of their shops and chanted anti-India slogans. Our boys had to shoot one or two to disperse the crowd. The wing as you know is now in the War Museum in Delhi.'

'Did Father have his uniform on that day?'

'Let the dead rest,' he said. 'At your age you must think about women.'

He moved closer. His breath fell on my face, smell of cardamom.

'Your father has become one with the glacier, Kip. It was not long after the President decorated his chest with the Param Vir Chakra, the highest decoration our army gives to the brave.'

'He fought two wars with the enemy.'

'Yes. And because of that the army wanted to make you an officer.'

I said nothing. I turned my gaze towards the bikes, which were leaning against a tree not far from us, his saddle higher than mine.

'But I have heard that you could not clear the medical exam, Kirpal. Is this true? Is this their indirect way? To make you a chef first, and then promote you? An officer's son will always become an officer. Certain things never change in our country.'

I surveyed his face and thought 'I am looking at eyes that have looked at my father.' There were things he knew about my father that he would never reveal to me.

'Is it possible?' I asked, moving away from him. 'My worst fear is that the glacier might release Father's body in the land of the enemy and — '

'No,' he interrupted. That was impossible. He drew a picture of the glacier on a torn sheet of paper. Then he asked me to label it in 'Inglish'.

'You see, Kip, the tongue of the glacier is in India and the whole mass is shifting slowly towards our side. His body will definitely be released on the soil of our country. The only way the body might transfer to Pakistan is if the glacier starts retreating very fast and becomes a part of the river, which is unlikely.'

'Nothing is unlikely,' I said.

'Certain things are unlikely,' he said and touched my cheek.

I asked him to withdraw his hand. Chef took a while.

'Not so long ago,' he said, 'there was an old Norwegian tourist who while trekking through the Himalayas found the body of his father at the foot of Siachen. The glacier had released

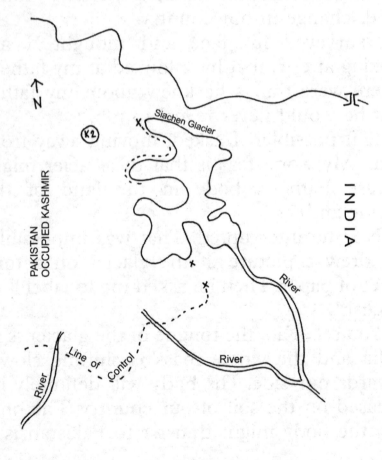

the body fully preserved. His father was much younger than him.'

'I read that news in the paper,' I said. 'Two days later the glacier released the body of a soldier whose plane crashed before the Partition.'

'Good news,' exclaimed Chef. 'The soldier belongs to India.'

'Do we know for sure?'

'Hundred percent, kid,' he said, pinching my cheek. I stood up and wiped my uniform.

'Your face turns color like the plane trees,' he said.

We biked down the hill, and bought eggs, goat meat, karam, lotus roots, and vegetables from the bazaar.

6

Autumn is not a season in India. In Kashmir autumn arrives in the month of October. Through the soot-coated kitchen window I would watch the chenar trees dance. They moved like dervishes in the wind. I had never seen autumn before. Both sides of the streets were lined by plane trees. The whole valley would burst into Technicolor. The leaves turned as they fell on the roofs and the streets, turning any surface into a red and yellow and orange carpet. The wind carried them, swirled them, then abandoned the leaves one by one. Contemplating their sadness I would forget my own, and I would forget, too, the Siachen Glacier. Even if blindfolded, I will still be able to detect the chenar leaves. I can't forget the smell of cut grass, and the smell of plane trees. How sad the trees look when shedding leaves, and yet how happy, as if trying to kiss the whole world. Autumn is not the end of happiness. It is the beginning.

★　★　★

I was almost twenty years old, bursting with energy and I had yet to sleep with a woman. Realistically, what were my chances? In the camp there were wives of other soldiers and officers. Outside the camp lived the Kashmiris. So there was no chance at all.

Often I would cycle past the Kashmiris' timber-framed houses and past children with runny noses and the old men with henna-dyed beards smoking hookahs. But it was rare to spot a woman. Then one day, standing by the banks of the river, I noticed a young woman washing apples. No sari, but loose drawstring pants and a loose knee-length robe, a pheran. Her breasts jiggled inside. The pheran was wet around her belly, the salwar was rolled up to the knees. Both feet inside the water, and the channel was clear and cold and transparent and very quiet. Now and then she stirred the quietness with the apples and her delicate feet. I observed her, standing on the rock. The nape of her neck was smooth and clean. Kashmiri women do not dress in a normal way. In summer the women wear light cotton pherans. In winter they prefer dark woolen ones made of pashmina. The garment is embroidered in front and on the edges. When it gets very cold the women tuck their arms inside. Some carry firepots close to their bellies (as if heavy with a child) and the arms of the pheran oscillate left and right like pendulums of time.

She turned only once and our eyes locked for a brief second.

'What are you going to do with the apples?' I asked.

She smiled, stepped out of the water and started heading towards the street behind the trees. She was more or less my age.

Next day, same time, I returned to the same rock by the river. Salaam, I heard a man's voice.

'Come have tea at our house.'

'Who are you?' I asked.

'I am her relative,' he said.

'Whose relative?'

'I am the brother of the woman you had a conversation with yesterday.'

'Hardly a conversation,' I said.

'Don't worry. I am a well-respected man with a very responsible job. I drive the city bus.'

'I have no time,' I said. 'My break is over.'

'Come for two minutes only.'

The man guided me through narrow cobble-stoned streets (with open sewer drains on both sides) to his house. Boys were playing cricket in the street. Just outside he requested me in good Urdu to remove my shoes. The moment we entered he said, 'Two teas.' We sat on a carpet with a variety of floral designs. Beautiful calligraphic scrolls hugged the walls, and the furniture smelled of pine wood. 'Are you married?' he asked. It was his first question. 'No,' I answered. 'Aha,' he said. 'You looked to me as if you were not married.'

It was then the woman entered the drawing room. She was carrying a tray. On a plate, which trembled on the tray, she had brought along tscvaru. The shortbread was coated with poppy seeds. She did not look at me directly. She bent low and served us tscvaru. Her hair was long and alive and for a moment I thought she was going to join us.

'The samovar is on,' she said and disappeared into the kitchen.

'I have never seen a samovar,' I said to the brother. 'May I observe it in the kitchen?'

'She'll bring the tea here only,' he said.

'Really I am in a hurry,' I said.

The man remained quiet. I imagined her in the kitchen with her samovar, something amazing that I heard came from the Russians.

'Does she go to college?' I asked.

'Sister was a brilliant student,' he said.

'What field?'

'Bee farmer,' he said.

'Bee farmer?'

'B. Pharma,' he said. 'Bachelor of Pharma-ceutical. She had to discontinue because of the *turmoil* in the valley.'

'I would like to get to know her,' I said. 'Perhaps I can go to cinema or theater with her?'

He cleared his throat and stared at me as if I had come from some other planet, and told me that the cinema houses (except the military theatre) had long been shut down because of the *turmoil*. Kashmir is not now what it used to be, he said.

The woman returned to the room and bent low and left the tea tray on a small table. This time she made a somewhat prolonged eye contact with me. Her face was very fair. Eyes cold blue. Lips, the color of apples.

'Fast,' said the brother.

She poured tea into two cups, chipped at the top. My cup *cracked* the moment it came in contact with hot fluid. I remember the sound of water being poured, the silence of water dripping on the carpet. But my hostess's face revealed no embarrassment. Keeping her gaze fixed on the carpet she recited a couplet in Urdu:

Es ghar ki kya deekh bhal karain, roz cheese koi nai toot jatea hai?
How does one take care of this house, every day some new thing breaks apart?

The poem cheered me up, and yet her brother looked angry. She ran to the kitchen and fetched a brand-new cup. It seemed the thing was meant for very special guests. I drank the kehva tea greedily. It was delicious! Strands of saffron floated on top, releasing the color. It had come right out of the samovar and the brew was strong. I detected crushed cardamoms, kagzee almonds, and asked myself: why is it that places with the worst possible hygiene manage to manufacture the best possible tea?

'The tea is la'zeez,' he said. 'Delicious!'

'Why is she not sitting with us?'

'She is in the kitchen,' he said.

'I, too, spend most of my time in kitchen,' I said.

'Let me be very upfront about your situation,' he said. 'I have *no objections*.'

'What do you mean *no objections*?'

'No objections to marriage.'

'Marriage?' I clarified. 'Whose marriage?'

'Yes, yes,' he said, 'let us have a *conversation*. If you want to marry her, I have no objections.'

The tea was very good.

He gulped down his cup. 'I do not like too much Indian *military* presence in the valley. Despite this I am happy *you* have a steady job. Will you marry my sister?'

49

'I need time,' I said.

'No problem,' he said.

I stood up with the cup in my hand and he rose to his feet. He pointed his index finger towards the calligraphy on the wall. I walked closer to read clearly.

'This word means peace,' I said.

'I am surprised,' he said.

'I attend Sunday language classes.'

I thought he was going to thank me for learning his language. But he didn't have the decency to do so, no meharbani, no shukriya, nothing; instead he started praising the language into which he was born, how *beautiful* it was, how *elegant*.

'Kashmiri is the language of poetry,' he said.

'There is no such thing as the language of poetry,' I corrected him. 'Poetry can be written in all languages. No language is inferior. When I peel an onion in the kitchen there is poetry in it.'

'You are not entirely wrong,' he said.

It was then I felt the pressing need to pose the question:

'So, you *do not* care about religion?'

'I hope you have no problem converting to Islam,' he said. 'Because that is absolutely necessary for the wedding. You must first convert to Islam. Of course when I

50

approached you by the river I knew you were born into a Sikh family. But I know one decent Sikh boy who converted because he fell in love with a Kashmiri Muslim girl.'

I took my last sip.

'Good tea,' he said. 'Wasn't the tea good?'

'The tea was excellent,' I said. '*Salaam-alaikum.*'

'*Valaikum-salaam*,' he said.

★   ★   ★

I hurried back to General Sahib's residence. There were more leaves on the street now than on the trees. The wind tossed them and turned them and swirled them and blew them back to the khaki barracks. Rubiya was playing barefoot on the lawns of the residence with her black dog. I felt like talking to her, but the ayah was also present.

The ayah was certainly attractive, a Goan. Her eyes glowed like pods of tamarind. The General's daughter was very attached to her. Because she had access to all the rooms in the residence the ayah thought she had fallen on this Earth as a superior being. She treated me as if I didn't matter; only a bit higher than the sweeper, who drank tea from a separate cup. She would shield Rubiya from all the male members of the staff, including Chef. But I

51

really felt for the girl because she was without a mother and her father was absent most of the time. Rubiya was not even allowed to order her own food. From a distance the sense I got was that Rubiya was shy, always hiding under the bed or table. But tell me, I would ask the ayah, what is the girl really like? This is not *your* concern, she would respond.

'Rubiya refuses to eat the red beans I cook for her?' I asked. We were standing just outside the kitchen.

'Razma reminds her of kidneys.'

'What is wrong with kidneys?'

'Kidneys make urine.'

'What?'

'Pee-pee,' she said.

'Please don't talk such things. I am cooking.'

'I must. The girl just can't digest your beans.'

★ ★ ★

Rubiya's gas problem was solved by adding heeng to the dish. The English word for heeng is asafetida. I like the sound of 'heeng' better. The ayah preferred 'asafetida' . . . One day she approached me on the verandah. She had a huge cleavage and her sari smiled with the weight of it. There was a little comb in her hand. I was plucking dhaniya leaves on the verandah, and the ayah asked me why I looked so unhappy. Is Rubiya sleeping in her room? I asked. Yes, yes. But we are talking about *you*, and she started combing her hair from side to side and probed me further about my unhappiness, and I told her to look down at the valley below. Look down at the parade ground, I said. See the troops marching in the parade ground. Young boys are learning techniques from older experienced boys. Learning warfare. Jumping. Crawling. Shooting. Aiming. Marching.

Then she asked me, what was it I wanted to learn *exactly*?

I said I *really* wanted to learn how to have sex, and perhaps someone like you could teach me? She stopped smiling. Have you gone crazy? she said.

I stepped out for a long walk by the river in the valley. Red leaves floated on the water, flowing as far as the mountains that belonged to the enemy. Later that night I drank rum in the barracks. A soldier told me: 'Your only chance, Kip, is with the nurse in the hospital. She is a *forward* woman. A man like you deserves a forward woman, Major. She is *ideal*, Major.'

I don't understand.

I-d-e-a-l W-o-m-a-n M-a-j-or.

53

Why am I thinking about these things? Life is withering away, and I should bring to mind only the essential matters. God. Reincarnation. Matters like that. Not food. Not women. Not even ravishing women. Not even women who understand the body, like the nurse. She took her afternoon breaks in the Mughal garden. One day without telling Chef I cycled all the way to say hello to her. There was a chill in the air. The garden was terraced, a royal pavilion in the middle, water flowed in straight lines and fell from one impatient chute to the next before entering the lake at the bottom. Locking my cycle by the gates I noticed she was standing on the uppermost terrace, not far from the ruined wall, smoking a cigarette. I waved. She beckoned me. The garden was filled with tourists and languages I didn't understand. She leaned against the wall as I walked closer. There was a brittle red-and-black leaf stuck in her hair.

'Did you finish your lunch already?' I asked.

'Generally I skip lunches,' she said.

She was wearing a pretty salwar-kameez with flowery designs, and I said that the kameez and the white hospital coat looked *funtoosh* on her, and she smiled and asked why I was wearing a bangle, and I explained that it was not a *bangle* at all, the thing on my right wrist was actually a steel bracelet. All

Sikh boys and girls wear the bracelet, I said. It looks *cool* on you, she said. What do you mean? I asked. In America, she explained, when something looks funtoosh on you, they say *it looks cool on you*. Thank you, I said and tried to hold her hand, but she frowned and said, 'Touching this way doesn't look nice.' I didn't know what to say, I felt I had done something very *uncool*, then for no reason I muttered a few words about the cold Kashmiri weather, and the sadness of Kashmir. This whole place is so beautiful, I said, and yet it is so sad. Look at the barren fruit orchards, the mountains, the lake which has been invaded by weeds. The temples, the mosques, the empty houses, the ruins — everything is sad. I sense a mingling of sadnesses here, I said. It seems as if all the people of Kashmir and all the people who come here, everyone is sad. It is not just a single person (like me) who is sad, rather the situation in the city sprouts the feeling of sadness in everyone. When one is unhappy one doesn't even enjoy the food one cooks, the basic things in life, I said. One forgets how to love, and life is so short. What are you talking about? she asked. Sadness, I said.

Back in the kitchen, I stood by the window. The plane trees were bare now. The words she had uttered *doesn't look nice* and *what* are *you* *talking* *about* and *it looks cool* left me anxious and happy at the same time, for there was still hope, for I had not lost her completely, for despite her lukewarm response she had not said a complete *no* and I felt a deep desire to transform the slim hope to reality.

That night in our bedroom Chef poured beer into two tall glasses. The beer was not bad at all. We clinked the glasses the way officers do. Cheers, I said.

'You speak such good Inglish,' he said. 'Were you trying to impress the nurse?'

'I was only talking.'

So he had seen us together.

'Nurses do not like softies. Inglish or no Inglish.'

'Me?'

'You still don't know how to handle a knife.'

'Sir, I will . . . work hard.'

'Look at me in the eye. Certain things cannot be changed, Kirpal. An officer's son can never stop being a softie. You see, when I was a boy I found certain smells disgusting. I was repelled by the smell of fenugreek and bitter gourd. Now I have overcome that repulsion, in fact I have come to love the very same smells I hated as a boy. But, certain smells continue to be repulsive.'

'Like what, sir?'

'Kashmiris,' he said. 'Badboo — '

I ignored him. To distract him I said, 'Sir, I would like to cook like you!'

He tasted the foam of beer, and flexed his muscles and the veins of his right forearm bulged. There was a tattoo on his arm, his name in green letters in Hindi. He wore a khaki shirt, the buttons open, underneath no banian and the hair on his chest was a forest of black-and-white curlicues.

'Do you want to replace me?'

'No, sir.'

'Replace me,' he said. 'I want you to learn all I know. The day your training is over, Gen Sahib will promote me. He has promised.'

'What rank would that be, sir, when you become an officer?'

'That of a captain,' he said, and put his tattooed arm around my shoulder, and stroked my cheek.

'When will my training end?' I asked.

Chef hopped on to his bed.

'The day you lose your virginity,' he said.

'Pardon me, Chef?'

'The smell of a woman is thousand times better than cooking the most sumptuous dinner, kid.'

'I would not know, Chef.' I felt embarrassed.

'Come sit next to me,' he said.

He took another swig of beer.

'Have you ever gone down on a woman?'

I lowered my gaze. He slapped my thigh.

'You see, when I was younger I found the smell down there disgusting. Now I have overcome that repulsion, in fact I have come to love the very same smells I hated when I was young.'

I gulped down my glass of beer without stopping for breath. He pulled his red journal from under the pillow and showed me a dirty picture.

'Look at this,' he said.

Below the sketch there were long passages in Hindi and Punjabi.

'Chef, what have you written in there?'

'None of your business,' he said. 'Pay attention to the picture!'

'I am looking,' I said.

'She is a memsahib,' he laughed.

'Yessir.'

'Did you ever kiss a memsahib?' he mumbled. 'Give me another Kingfisher.'

When he fell asleep I surveyed the empty beer glasses. Chef groaned in his bed. His naked chest heaved up and down. There was a strange rhythm to his muscles. I spent the night eating berries. In Kashmir everything tastes of fruit. The days tasted of apples and the nights of bittersweet berries. I ate them very slowly, one by one.

7

We were preparing mutton yakhni. Dipping
fingers in the marinade. The air in the room
carried the scent of star anise. Turn the flame
on high, he said. Now, he said. One by one I
dropped the half-brown, half-crimson pieces
of meat into the degchi. Stir, he said. The
mutton must never stick to the bottom. Chef,
when do I add yoghurt? Not now, he said and
explained the difference between *precision*
and *estimation*. Then he wiped his hands on
my apron. I felt uncomfortable, but kept
stirring. Cook without fear of failure, Kirpal.
But you must never fail. Take good care of
your hands, Kirpal. He stared at my hands
while teaching. If you lose the use of your
hands you will be useless in the kitchen.
Don't ever think of touching a memsahib. If
you want to keep your fingers intact simply
keep away from memsahibs. Observe them
from distance only.

Now, he said. Now you add the yoghurt to
the pot. Yessir. I followed his command, and
covered the degchi with a lid. He stroked my
cheek and started humming German music.
The music was beautiful. His hands moved

up and down as if they were guiding invisible instruments. Then he stopped. I mean it, Kip. Take good care of your hands, kid. Not like the Sikh guitarist. The guitarist? I asked. Yes, yes; he cleared his throat. The Sikh guitarist belonged to 72nd Battalion, 5th Mountain Division. The man was blessed with the most elegant fingers, and he used to play for Colonel Tagore's wife at the colonel's house. The colonel, said Chef Kishen, was keen on young men and he used to hang out at a special room in the Officers' Mess and he had no problems leaving his young wife alone with the guitarist who would play for her till the wee hours of the morning. They had no children, the colonel and his wife, but in the beginning I simply could not believe that man's fondness for boys. The colonel (who was a major then) would find boys in the hospital. He would visit the doctor during the season of recruitment or just before the troops were dispatched to the front. He would stand next to the doctor during the medical examination and survey the naked bodies of hundreds of troops — optimistically — with a smile on his face. But his eyes had indescribable sadness in them, said Chef Kishen. He would move his gaze from head to toe, from toe to head, and after the chest measurements he would ask each one of the soldiers their age and the reason for joining the army, and he would try to persuade the boys to quit the battalions and return home. This, said Chef Kishen, was the psychological examination. I cannot even begin telling you how I felt the day the colonel fixed his gaze on my chest (I was a young man then and I had felt the heat of the colonel's desire on my body and a part of me had felt really flattered because he had desired my body but I naturally felt no desire for him) and a chill went through my spine, but at that very moment I noticed the colonel's gaze move to the troop standing next to me. I must confess, said Chef, my neighbor was far more good-looking and handsome than me and as a result the colonel simply lost all interest in me and started persuading the soldier to quit the army and not go to the front and when the recruit responded with clarity that he was going to do his duty for the sake of our great country, the colonel patted thrice on the man's back. The colonel's eyes welled up there and then. Days later, said Chef Kishen, I was the one — new to everything — who discovered the Sikh guitarist in bed with the colonel's beautiful wife and now that I think about it I should have not stirred things up. The guitar was lying on the floor. The guitarist was in a white banian only and she wearing a petticoat only. I remember her smooth-looking body down to the tassels of her petticoat. The burgundy color of her sweaty blouse, which was clinging to the guitar. They did not see me. If I had sealed my lips the regiment gossip would not have started, the rumor would not have spread inside and outside the barbed wires like orange forest fire and things would not have followed the ugly course they did. General Sahib had not moved to Kashmir yet. The one before him, General Jagmohan, had the guitarist arrested and in the prison they chopped off the top of his fingers and afterwards commanded him to play the guitar, which he did. The colonel I heard later, continued Chef, had begged the General to spare the guitarist's fingers. (The guitarist looked a bit like you. I am not one of those who believes that all men in turbans look exactly like each other, but your face, Kirpal, has a striking resemblance.) To this day I think the colonel did the begging because the colonel and his wife had made a secret pact: the colonel was interested in men and he was going to sleep with them despite the marriage, and his wife was interested in other men and she was going to sleep with them despite the marriage. This was their *arrangement*, which I did not know, around the time. Because of my intervention, said Chef Kishen, the colonel's interest in men was revealed and afterwards he found it difficult to face certain persons in the army. When Colonel Tagore died 'accidentally' in the war with Pakistan some of us knew that his death was not an accident. His wife, the young widow, was pursued by a major (who is a colonel now) and exactly eleven months later she yielded and the two of them got married. Tonight they are coming to dinner. Who? I asked. Colonel Chowdhry and his wife, he said.

'Tonight, from behind that curtain, I will show you the real thing.' Chef cleared his throat. 'The real memsahib,' he said.

'Tonight?'

'Yes, observe her attitude. She speaks polished Inglish. And observe her nakhra. The way she holds a fork.'

8

Everything is ready, almost ready, in the kitchen. Fumes are rising from simmering pots. Soup is cream of corn. Starter is sheekh kebab. Main course is seven items, including pork in mango-coriander sauce. Memsahib is vegetarian, Chef tells me. Navrattan paneer and dal makhni have been prepared especially for her. Lady Fingers are also for her. Biryani, kakori and fish are for the colonel. Trout is ready — from Dachigam in the morning.

Evening approaches. Tonight the real memsahib is coming. The sun reddens the kitchen walls before it sets in the enemy's land.

Everything is ready.

General Sahib stands on the verandah, hands clasped behind him. He is an inch or two above six feet and he always stands in this manner. The black American suit gives him a stately air, the red scarf on his neck depicts a leaping leopard. There is a fresh shaving mark just below his left cheek. His skin has an oily sheen, no wrinkles yet. Everything about him is what I had imagined to see in a General, even his eyes, which are at once intimidating and filled with compassion. He bends his neck, listening to the sound of footsteps on the gravel path. The guests are approaching.

The colonel, a short man wearing a black beret, walks a little ahead of his wife. She has Bombay actress good looks, but he is a bit on the heavier side. He looks restrained but angry as if already tonight someone has offended him deeply.

The two men shake hands firmly.

Sahib kisses the memsahib on her cheek, which is red because of make-up. She giggles. Says something in English.

'India and Pakistan all right?' asks General Sahib.

'Both of us are very well, sir!' says the colonel.

'I don't believe a word!' says Sahib.

'No. Please don't believe him,' says Memsahib and giggles.

'Is there anything I can do to help?' Sahib guides them to the living room.

'More fire power,' says the colonel, now looking more relaxed.

'Darling, stop it,' she says with a sparkle in her eyes.

She is wearing silk. The sari clings to the curves of her body, tight, as if purely out of desire.

Inside, Chef explains the meaning. 'Gen

Sahib calls all married couples as India and Pakistan.'

'But who is Pakistan?'

'Women are.'

There are three sofas in the drawing room, and a grand fireplace with glowing red coal. The painting of the dead woman looks down at the guests from the wall. Not far from the painting there is a glass cabinet. The artillery mementoes inside the cabinet demand one's attention. Next to the mementoes are bottles of finest quality rum and scotch, and Kingfisher beer.

She sinks in the sofa, the real memsahib.

Chef and I are standing just behind the gap in the curtain. He is holding a sharp knife; he keeps wiping the blade with his apron. Now and then he points a finger. At first I find it hard to observe the colonel's wife properly. All I can see clearly is the back of her blouse.

'Where is the little one?' she asks.

'Rubiya, your Aunty and Uncle have arrived,' says Sahib a bit loudly.

Rubiya is in her room with the ayah.

'Papa, I am trying to commit suicide,' she shouts from her room.

General Sahib laughs.

'She learns these words. Don't know from where. She doesn't even know the meaning of 'suicide'. Two days ago she told the ayah that her mother actually committed a suicide.'

India and Pakistan laugh.

The colonel rubs his hands.

'Whiskey?'

'With soda, sir.'

The colonel clears his throat.

'Your wife was very beautiful, sir.' He admires the painting; so does the memsahib.

'She was a coastal woman.'

'The beauty of Kashmiri women, sir, is overrated. Real beauty belongs to Indian women, especially from the coastal regions, as you very rightly said. Coastal women are *real*. They have *real* features. They may be darker, but with impressive features. That is why they get crowned Miss World, and Miss Universe also. Our Aishwarya Rai, sir!'

'Kashmiri women here have a delicate beauty,' says General Sahib. 'The kind of beauty hard for Indian women to match. They are fair, they are lovely. What else can I say? I disagree with you, colonel.'

The two men look at the colonel's wife.

'What does *Pakistan* say?' asks the General.

She wants to say something, but decides against it. She smiles tactfully, changes her seat. Her heels click when she moves next to Gen Sahib on the sofa. Sahib sips his drink.

'But to us, Patsy, you are the one most beautiful,' he says. The General touches her naked arm. Then he laughs and she, too, giggles and squeezes his hand.

The colonel chews his lips. 'A thing of beauty is a joy forever,' he says after a long pause.

The curtain flaps on my face.

'What do you think about Memsahib?' asks Chef, wiping the knife with his apron.

'She is all right,' I say.

She is wearing a low-cut blouse. Observe the shape, whispers Chef. She drinks two or three glasses of port and, I observe, the drinking is making her sad. The two sahibs raise their voices reminiscing about younger days when they were in the Military Academy, where they had been trained alongside batch-mates who were now running the enemy army in Pakistan. Memsahib's nails are long and red and her hair is red too because of henna.

Chef wipes his hands on my apron and takes a mirchi and chops it like a surgeon and garnishes the Wagah biryani. *Smell it, kid.* Jee, sir . . . He applies a sizzling tarka to dopiaza and yells at server: Is the table ready? Chef hurries back to his position behind the curtain and with his finger makes me taste his new invention, the Mhow chutney. Then he puts his arm around my shoulder.

Memsahib flips through a foreign maga-zine, which has many photographs. She is comparing herself to the photos.

It is our time to come to existence, Chef tells me. We come to existence only to carry out orders. He parts the curtains briefly and enters the drawing room. There is a rhythm in his legs. He clicks his heels.

'Dinner is ready to be served, sir.'

'Dinner, Memsahib.'

Gen Sahib and India-Pakistan move to the table. Back in the kitchen, ghee sizzles and the air tastes pungent and Chef orders the assistant to start slapping more naans in the tandoor and phulkas on the griddle. Perfect puffed-up circles. No maps of India, he warns.

Yessir.

The guests keep an eye on the General's plate. When he eats fast, they eat fast. When he slows down, they slow down. Sahib keeps an eye fixed on Memsahib's face, even while chewing the lamb. He is liking the Rogan Josh. Sometimes his fork makes circles in the air, sometimes his knife hits the plate like artillery. But, he is liking the lamb. She eats with her mouth shut. She stops chewing now and then and flashes a smile.

Memsahib will stop eating only when he stops, says Chef. The General is aware of this. So he will keep eating until he is sure that Memsahib is almost finished.

They talk about classical music, beekeeping, carpets, silkworms, diameter of the most ancient plane tree, absence of railways in Kashmir, loathsome Kashmiris, and picnics in the Mughal gardens. Also about Nehru when he was the PM: an army helicopter would fly to his residence in Delhi with Kashmiri spring water. They pause just before their conversation drifts towards hometowns, educational institutions, well-settled brothers and sisters. Then one of them mentions death: the soldier who killed his own sergeant, the Major who hanged himself at the border, and the young Captain killed recently during the Pakistani shelling on the glacier.

'Excellent biryani.'

The napkin touches the General's lips.

Chef shoves the server in, bearing finger bowls. He returns for the dessert tray. Halva. Ashrafi. Jalaybee. Crescents of watermelon, and aloobukharas and peaches and strawberries. The colonel's wife has become unusually silent. She closes her eyes and breaks out of silence slowly. Not a single Kashmiri fruit can make me forget the taste of a mango, she says.

'The best way to eat a mango is to suck it,' says the colonel.

'Yes, yes,' says Gen Sahib.

'Every time I eat a mango I think of Major Iqbal Singh's Partition story,' she says. 'And that Muslim woman who saved his life . . . '

Memsahib stops talking in mid-sentence.

The two men avoid the subject.

(Father never told me anything about someone saving his life in 1947.)

I look at Chef. Those real Pakistani women can't even save a dog, he says. Memsahib watches too many films, he whispers.

The three of them are sitting on the sofas again.

'More dessert for Pakistan?' asks the General.

'No,' she says.

'Pakistan must have more?'

'No, no,' she says.

General Sahib starts the records.

Time passes.

It passes very quickly, then slows down. Music makes time pass slowly.

How could the woman save my father's life? I ask myself.

Sahib raises his voice. 'Kishen,' he beckons.

Chef dashes in with fennel seeds and tea on tray.

'Food was all right, Sahib?' he inquires.

'Excellent trout and biryani.'

'Was it Hyderabadi?'

'*A-One* Rogan Josh!'

'Good brinjals!'

'Local produce?'

'Many things came from our own vegetable garden, Memsahib.'

'I have only one complaint,' she says.

'Yes, Memsahib?'

She is stirring her tea.

'Did the knife touch meat? I smelled non-veg in paneer.'

The General stares at Chef.

'Sorry, Memsahib. If you would allow me, I will check with the trainee cook.'

'The Sikh chap?' asks the General.

'Sir.'

'Sir, my wife has a sharp nose,' says the colonel apologetically. He wipes dust off his green regimental blazer.

The General is not looking very happy.

Chef dashes back to the kitchen. He pulls me up by holding my ears and stares at me angrily and drops me on the floor with a thud. I murmur an apology. He shoves me towards the tandoor, parts the curtain, and returns.

'Separate knives were used, Memsahib,' he assures her. 'The trainee says he added mushroom water. The *non-wage* taste was coming from mushrooms.'

I breathe a sigh of relief.

'Who is this Sikh in the kitchen?' asks the colonel's wife.

'Major Iqbal's son,' says Gen Sahib, hesitating.

'Our Iqbal's boy in the kitchen?'

'Don't worry. He is on the fast track.'

'I see,' she says.

I watch the ayah enter the room with Rubiya. The child is in a pink frock, looks sickly. The ayah forces Rubiya to say *good evening, uncle, good evening, aunty.* She acts shy. Sahib scolds her not to be shy. Only a minute ago you were going to commit suicide, and now, my sweet *pisti*, what happened to your tongue? Suddenly the girl says: Colonel, uncle can help me! Uncle can help me! How? Asks Sahib. Uncle is a fat man, says Rubiya. Bad manners, says Sahib. Uncle has thick fingers, he can choke me to suicide. Don't talk like that, says Sahib.

'He is fat, uncle is fat.'

'Sing the National Anthem, Rubiya,' says ayah. The girl pauses, then does exactly what she has been told. She sings *jana gana mana* in a baby voice and runs and hides under the table.

Memsahib wants to say something to her husband but changes her mind and turns her gaze towards the curtain. She starts walking towards us. *Pakistan is going to invade the kitchen,* whispers Chef. He shoves me towards the clay oven and parts the curtains and smiles a fake smile. Memsahib would like to have a word with the trainee.

I lift my hands and fold them to say namasté. My brain fogs up. I bow. She says something in Hindi, I respond in good English. My attention moves from her feet to her ringed finger. She is standing very close to me now, a very tough moment, and Chef doesn't utter a word, he observes with tiger eyes. Memsahib in her convent accent inquires about my hometown and education and thousand other things, including, if I was really Iqbal Singh's son, and I feel like talking to her more and more, and I want to ask her about my father's Partition story, but meanwhile I am liking her feminine presence in the kitchen, and the old vaccine mark on her upper arm. She is wearing a sleeveless blouse, but abruptly she turns, her sari spins like a top, and her high heels start clicking and it hits me hard the sound of her heels clicking as she returns to the drawing room. Before she leaves she says: come see me sometime. Chef scolds me: why did you talk to the memsahib in Inglish? Rubiya is still in the drawing room with the ayah. Memsahib sits next to the motherless girl. She strokes the girl's ruddy cheek. The girl is the spitting image of the dead woman in the painting. The men are not paying attention to the girl or the memsahib. Sahib is talking, the colonel is listening. Now Sahib is listening, the colonel is talking. Conversation turns to Kashmir. Conversation always turned to Kashmir. The air in the room grows absolutely still.

Colonel: 'Sir, the way these people live.'

Colonel's wife: 'Darling . . . what do you mean?'

Colonel: 'If I may say so, sir. Each bloody Kashmiri has a bloody second wife.'

Colonel's wife: 'This means there must be twice as many women in Kashmir?'

General: 'Your wife does have a point.'

Colonel: 'No, sir. The brides come to Kashmir from bloody Bangladesh. And they bring along bloody men from bloody Islam, who are in touch with militants in Afghanistan and Pakistan, and they have occupied the bloody mosques, sir. They want bloody azadi, sir.'

Colonel's wife: 'The girl! Rubiya is listening.'

Her husband stands up abruptly and walks to the window.

Colonel: 'Outside it is very dark, sir. *Array baytah! You sing soooo well. You are a big girl now* — If I may say so, sir, the way the bloody bastards think — '

Colonel's wife: 'Shhh! The girl.'

Colonel: 'Sir, I love my India, sir . . . *Array baytah! What will you become when you*

75

grow really big? Tell me?'

Rubiya: 'Suicide.'

Colonel: 'Jokes apart, *baytah*. What will you really do?'

Rubiya: 'Go to Amay-ree-ka.'

Colonel's wife: 'Why so?'

Rubiya: 'Papa says so.'

Colonel: 'America is an astonishing country, sir. The doctor's daughter studies there at NYU. She loves it.'

Colonel's wife: 'Let's leave. We all love a good night's sleep. Don't we, darling?'

She giggles.

Colonel: 'Let me tell General sir one last thing, darling. I have found the perfect solution to deal with Pakistan, sir! Now that we've the N-weapon, it is very simple . . . I shared my idea with Mr. Ghosh, sir, but he didn't seem to get it . . . . Few nights ago, sir, I woke on my bed thinking the idea. Why don't we — and I am just thinking, sir — why not drill a hole in the glacier, bury the bomb inside, the way we do it in the desert sands, sir, and blow it up? The glacier would melt and millions and billions of liters of water will flow to their side and flood our enemy out of existence, sir?'

General: 'But, colonel. The enemy too has an N-weapon.'

Colonel: 'We'll do it first, sir.'

Colonel's wife: 'Darling, you and your ideas.'

'Please allow us, sir, to take our leave.'

'It was a delight.'

'Delighted, sir.'

'Good night.'

'Good night, sir.'

'Good night, uncle. Good night, aunty.'

'Good night, *baytah*!'

'Good night.'

The colonel and his wife departed. It took them a long time to say bye-bye, but eventually they departed. The General waved them off from the verandah. They lived close by, and they used torch lights walking on the narrow pebbled path. I was standing outside the kitchen taking a little break to try and settle myself, and overheard their conversation. The colonel's ideas about the glacier had made me very worried.

'Come on, darling, I know there is something *else* bugging you.'

'Now you have spoiled my chances of getting promoted.'

'Don't say that.'

'Why did you say the thing about the knives?'

'Darling — don't you get the point?'

'You have destroyed me.'

'Darling, come on.'

'Don't say dar-ling war-ling. Did not you see the General was silent after you said that nonsense?'

'He likes you.'

'Now I will never become a Brigadier.'

'But, darling, why did you run to the window so abruptly?'

'The view.'

'Don't lie. Do you think I do not know? You disappeared because . . . Do you think I do not know why you ran to the window and laughed so loudly and banged your fist against the table?'

'There is nothing wrong with conceal-ment.'

'A fart, darling? One must simply say *excuse me* the way one says before sneezing, and do it.'

'Like the General? I must say he is more honest.'

'Down to his farting. Darling.'

Their voices receded and the torch lights became little dots and were gone. Sounds of crickets took over. Bats and wolves reclaimed their territory. I saw the night humming with stars. I had never heard a married couple talking privately. They talked like civilians. Of farts and farting.

The kitchen was still filled with her nice smell. I found it difficult to express my feelings to Chef, so I made tea quickly and thanked him — as he was waiting for it — for saving my ass. To make up for my error, I shared the conversation with him, the exact exchange that took place between India and Pakistan. I mimicked the memsahib in English. But he grew unusually silent.

'Something wrong, Chef?'

'No Inglish.'

He started slurping tea noisily.

'What is wrong with English?'

'No Inglish!' he yelled at me.

Normally he lost his temper in the kitchen when the assistants licked their fingers or picked noses while marinating. I will ban you from the kitchen, he would yell. He banned Biswas, who was dumb like a cabbage, and Thapa, who scratched his groin while preparing dough. Ramji left because he was caught reading porn. (Later we found that he would also frequent the red-light district of the city to sleep with Muslim women.) Barring a few exceptions Chef was very lenient with me. But that day he simply lost it. He started cursing me. All because of Inglish. English came, and became a wall between us.

I had made a minor error, nothing in comparison to the error he had made. *I refused to serve tea to the Muslim officer.* He would repeat the story often when in an exceptionally good mood. In pure Hindi he would brag: *I refused tea to that man*. Several times when I was his apprentice I intended to ask why he had *really* done so. Was it just because of the *smell?* Would he still do so? What about the gardener, Agha? Did he dislike Agha, too, because he was a Muslim? But I could never gather the courage to pose the question.

I must be a weak character, I say to myself on this train.

9

In Srinagar whenever Colonel Chowdhry was away on border duty, during his long absences I would go out of my way to walk past his residence. There was an old plane tree in the garden with a rope swing attached to a high branch. Sometimes the convex swing would move on its own in the wind, and sometimes Memsahib would make it move with enormous force, her feet touching the ground now and then. To this day I can't forget her perfect feet, stained a little by the soil of Kashmir.

But there was something that troubled me whenever I looked at her or thought about her in my room. The sound of a guitar would echo in my head. I would try to conjure up the guitarist and his chopped fingers making love to the memsahib. A chill would go through my spine. Before her I had not experienced such a combination of fear and desire, and because I am a weak man the fear started swelling and the desire started shrinking. What saved me from that fear was a sudden bout of indigestion. The diarrhea took me to the hospital and there I encountered the nurse again, and all my desire towards

Memsahib transferred towards the nurse, now that I think about it, just like a few months earlier all my desire for the nurse had transferred towards the memsahib. The nurse's feet resembled the memsahib's, her hands, her entire body was almost like Memsahib's. Only difference: the nurse was a little dark, the color of cassia.

But.

I am jumping ahead of myself.

I did gather courage once, I did walk into Colonel Chowdhry's house once. I was under the impression he was away, but the man was home. Both he and his wife received me on the lawn. She asked me to sit down in the chair, but I looked at the colonel and his face didn't approve that I accept her offer. Lower ranks are not supposed to sit with commissioned officers, even if one happens to be the brother of the officer in question. I kept standing, hands clasped behind my back. It is good you came, said the wife. She was also standing. The reason I came, I said, looking her in the eye, is because I would like to hear Father's Partition story. Father never told me the details.

Yes, I thought so, she said. I think about you often since our meal at the Gen's.

'Who? This boy Kirpal?' interrupted the colonel.

'No, no. Major Iqbal,' she said. 'He was the silent type, he rarely opened up. This happened before I met you. Once my ex-husband and I invited Iqbal for dinner. God knows what it was really, perhaps the combination of food and drink and music made the Major open up that evening, but when conversation turned to the Partition he grew silent again. I poured him another drink.'

The colonel's wife stopped briefly and sat down in the chair. Why don't you two sit down as well? she said, hitting her forehead with her delicate hand. The colonel sat down immediately, and I sat on the ground. But she stood up and stepped towards me and extended her hand and helped me move to the empty chair. The colonel looked in the other direction. At first I felt uncomfortable in the chair, but it became increasingly clear to me that she wanted to treat me like a son. This is how she related my father's story to me in the colonel's angry presence.

Month of August, 1947. India had just been partitioned by the British. Thousands of Sikhs in the city of Lahore suddenly found themselves on the wrong side of the new border, your father, Major Iqbal, told me. I was nine, he said. I used to tie my long hair into a knot on my head; I had not started wearing a turban yet. I used to cover the knot

83

with a tiny patch of muslin (my mother had devised a rubber band mechanism to hold the patch tight). Breakfast was ready, and my uncles and aunts and grandparents were all gathered in the living room. I can see the carpeted floors, I can see the velvet sofas, and through the window I can see the mango tree in the yard. Grandmother had prepared aloo-parathas in the kitchen, she tried to persuade Mother not to send me to the class because of tension between communities, but Mother said education was important. I ran all the way to the school with my heavy satchel only to find a big notice at the gates. School was cancelled. The city was on fire. The cinema halls were closed, and there was fire and smoke all over and Hindu, Sikh, and Muslim bodies were burning everywhere, and I ran back to our house through charred streets. When I got home, I found all the doors open and the water faucet running for no particular reason. In the living room, on the velvet sofas and on the red carpets, I found the chopped-off heads of my grandparents and mother and siblings and other family members; the killers had gathered them up, and piled them up neatly, as if they were market fruit.

That evening, I boarded the train to India. But it ended up it was the wrong train, said your father. It was filled with Muslims. The train had come to the newly created Pakistan from India and it was not returning to India. He said, I cannot forget the look on the faces of my fellow passengers, it was as if they were worried for me. I was very afraid, but I tried not to show it. I kept staring at the woman sitting on the seat across from me. She stood out from the human mass around her, she was eating a mango, sucking it (that is the right word), and now and then drops kept falling on her green toenails. She was wearing heels, and three layers of her clothing were touching her feet, the innermost circle or the hem belonging to her white petticoat, the second hem belonging to her red sari and the outermost belonging to her black burqa. Her face was not covered, but her head and the rest of the body was covered by the black burqa. Her hands and feet were not covered, and they appeared so liberated. The three circles or the three hems of petticoat, sari and burqa were swelling and shrinking in the wind, the train window was open and the wind was hitting us all a bit violently.

The train stopped at a crowded platform. The wind stopped as well; now the air in the carriage grew hot and stagnant and oppressive. Through the window another train was visible on the other side of the platform. The

85

carriages were painted red or simply rusty, with as many people inside as there were on the roof. On the platform five or six Muslims with naked swords were asking regular passengers if they had seen a Hindu or a Sikh on the train. The woman stopped eating her mango. She started staring at me, so hard it appeared her eyes were going to explode. Suddenly she grabbed my right wrist and pulled me towards her and shoved me quickly under her seat. I was not a very tall nine-year-old, so the squeeze was all right. The voices were now moving up and down the aisle of our train demanding Sikhs and Hindus. The woman started on the mango again. Drops started falling down, she was sucking it. The men were now extremely close to our compartment. For a moment I felt the woman was going to hand me over to them. She began tapping her heels and this terrified me under the seat. Why was she tapping? Why was she drawing attention? Were the heels trying to convey something to me? She tapped forcefully one last time and lifted the three hems of her burqa-sari-petticoat a bit in the air, then higher, and it was then I understood. I crawled inside. She immediately lowered the garments; now they touched the floor again. Suddenly it grew very dark around me.

Where is the Sikh boy? demanded the mob. From the platform we definitely noticed a boy on this train, said a voice loudly.

What Sikh? said a passenger.

The men were suspicious and opened up several suitcases and looked under the seats. I heard them, I could not see a thing. I was trapped inside absolute darkness. It was like being in a movie theater alone, wrapped by the white screen, and no movie on. It was as if the real movie was happening in the world outside the theater. The woman kept eating her mango. Drops kept falling. No other passenger in the compartment said a word. I imagine they simply turned their heads in the other direction. They all were Muslims. When the train stopped again it was very dark and I crawled out from under her and she quickly untied the knot on my head and made my hair tumble down to look like a girl. This is all I can do, she said, I can do nothing more for you. Allah will protect you now. He will protect you. She kissed me on both cheeks, gave me a little food and walked me to the refugee camp on the edge of the city.

This story, said the colonel's wife, I don't think I would have shared with you if you had not asked me the details. I will not be able to sleep tonight, she said.

Memsahib was shaking now. My gaze

remained fixed on her shoes. To this day I don't understand, Kirpal, why your father shared this painful story. I recall when he was sharing the details it was as if he was not there, it was as if he did not care if we were there or not. Normally men censor certain parts of a story when in the presence of a woman, but Iqbal was elsewhere that evening and to him it did not matter if I was listening or not.

'Listen, my boy,' said the colonel, 'it is time you go back to General Sahib's residence.'

'Sir.' I stood up and clicked my heels.

Memsahib ran indoors. I could not, therefore, say a proper shukriya to her. I have never been able to do what I really wanted to do. I am so weak.

10

Being a Sikh I am interested in hair. Some of my most sensuous memories are not connected to food at all. They are about hair. The way my mother would wash it, oil it, massage it, comb it, braid it, and tie a knot on top of my head. My hair was long and black and curly and whenever I dried it outdoors the wind would turn my head into a vortex. I cut my hair short fifteen years ago. But, during my time in Kashmir (the first four years) I had it long and used to tie a black turban. Sikhs believe in the holy book, the Adi Granth, and ten masters, Guru Nanak the first one and Guru Gobind Singh the last one. No one knows what the gurus really looked like, but in calendars they appear as if lost in deep meditation, unaware of the bright halos behind their Sufi-style turbans. Their beards are black or gray, but always long and flowing gracefully.

In Kashmir I tried to buy the Prophet Mohammed calendar. There was no such thing, I was told. It was hard to conjure him up. Every time I tried he would resemble one of the Sikh gurus.

In Srinagar, in the mosque with a single minaret, there was a strand of the Prophet's hair. It had been transported in a vial to Kashmir (in the luggage of a holy man) two or three centuries ago. Thousands of people gathered every year on a special day to be blessed by the holy relic. At first I thought the hair in the vial belonged to the head of the Prophet, but Chef corrected me. It comes from the Prophet's beard, he said.

If I have forgotten certain details from that time it is because I rarely got any sleep those days. The mosque was the holiest in Kashmir, but it had been hijacked by a group of militants, who used to gather in the hamaam to talk *azadi*.

The vial was kept under heavy security. But one day it disappeared. We read about the theft in the papers. The Kashmiris took to the streets in millions demonstrating against our country, blaming our leaders. Government buildings and vehicles were set on fire and the situation got out of hand.

My thoughts during those days of demonstrations kept turning to the colonel's wife. On the third day of the demos I gathered the courage to walk again to her residence, but the orderly told me that Memsahib was in the living room taking dance lessons from an instructor. I waited on the lawns. Their dark forms, visible through the window, whirled and spun, but I could not hear the steps. 'Kip,' she beckoned me finally on the verandah.

I folded my hands by way of greeting.

'Why did you come?'

'Are you disappointed?' I asked.

'No, no.'

'I have come to talk to you.'

'Talk to me?'

'Yes.' I hesitated for a moment. 'You don't look happy,' I said.

'Perhaps you have come to look at my kitchen?'

'Yes, yes, Memsahib.'

'Come in then.'

We passed through the living room. On the sofa a familiar man was sitting, the General's ADC. Seeing him my heart froze with terror, but I saluted anyway. He was wearing a French-cuff shirt and his shoes looked expensive and gleamed with confidence.

'Kip has come to inspect our kitchen,' she told him.

'I see,' he said, staring at me.

I followed her. There was nobody in the kitchen.

She stood next to the fridge and I next to the sink.

'We don't have much time,' she said. 'Now tell me — '

'Yes, Memsahib.'

'What have you heard about me?'

'Nothing,' I said.

'Tell me.'

'Nothing.'

'Liar,' she said. 'Your father was different.'

'So far nothing, Memsahib.'

'In that case soon you will start hearing things.'

'Yes, Memsahib.'

'I am like your Aunty,' she said.

'Yes, Memsahib.'

'Understand?'

'I do.'

'What did you hear?'

'If I hear things about you I will shut my ears.'

'You will shut your ears?'

'Yes, yes, Memsahib.'

'Show me how.'

I put fingers in my ears. I felt like a child.

'Shut your eyes as well,' she said.

I did exactly as I was told. I closed my eyes.

I heard her steps approaching me. Yet I felt uncertain. Then I felt her sari touch my shirt, and for a brief second she stabbed me with her pointed breasts. Then she stepped back and started slapping my face with the back of her hand. Left cheek. Right. Left again.

'Aunty!' I opened my eyes.

'Don't return,' she said. 'You are like a son to me.'

She rushed to the next room and said something inane to the ADC and they resumed the dance lessons.

I took the long way home to General Sahib's residence. Wet inside my pants, I felt like running. Instead, I slowed down. The chants and slogans of the Kashmiris demonstrating in the city kept insulting my ears, and I could not shut them out.

★ ★ ★

Two days later in the kitchen. I watched from behind the curtain, General Sahib was alone in the dining room with the colonel's wife. She was looking beautiful, her voice carried on waves of laughter. The colonel was supposed to be there, too, both had been invited, but Sahib dispatched him for an emergency law-and-order meeting with the Police Chief and the Governor.

The English they were speaking was fluent, with good idiom. Lunch was ready. Kebabs and rumali rotis. They were about to start when the red phone rang. Chef, he was standing close to the phone, answered.

'General Kumar's residence.'

Sahib: 'Who is it?'

Chef: 'Sir, the Prime Minister's secretary is on the line . . . the PM would like to talk to you . . . Matter is urgent, sir.'

Sahib: 'Is he on the line?'

Chef: 'Sir, the secretary will now tell the PM you are available. She has asked me, sir, to tell you not to move away from the phone, sir.'

For ten minutes there was absolute silence in the residence. It was hard for the colonel's wife to remain silent, but she too was silent.

Chef walked to the dining table on the tips of his toes to cover the dishes. That was the loudest sound during those ten minutes.

The secretary called again.

Chef: 'PM is on the line, sir.'

He stood glued to the dining table during the phone conversation. Later Chef shared with us in the kitchen the key details. The PM had basically told the General to locate and restore the holy relic to its proper place within forty-eight hours, no questions asked. The police failed to deliver so I am asking the army to take over, the PM had said.

Never before had the General looked so worried and anxious, Chef told us back in the kitchen. Sahib's face acquired the look of a man who had just been ordered (for the first time in his life) to slaughter a little goat. He scratched his head, plucked his hair while talking on the phone.

'Sir,' said the General to the PM. 'We will do our best, sir. Yes, sir . . . No, sir . . . It will be done, sir.' Right after the call ended he picked up the kebab on the table and for a long time kept moving the thing from left to right in his mouth without swallowing it.

'What now?' asked the colonel's wife.

Sahib kept working on the kebab.

★ ★ ★

No one to this day knows how and where the vial containing the relic was found. But after forty-eight hours calm was restored. The army faced one more hurdle. Before the relic could be installed in the mosque, it had to be validated.

The mosque named five holy imams to validate the holy relic. They were flown to Srinagar on DC-3 Dakota planes. Their job was to determine if the hair in the vial was authentic.

The General's ADC asked us in the kitchen to prepare a proper meal for the clerics. It is important to make them appreciate the high quality of our dishes. The ADC stared right through me during the conversation. Chef told mc after: this is your *real* test, kid. The recruitment test was a fake. At this critical moment in my career and your career and General Sahib's career, and at this critical juncture of Kashmir's relationship with India, what food would you prepare?

'Authentic Kashmiri,' I suggested.

'In that case,' he said, 'we will have to become Muslims.'

'Convert to Islam?'

'Of course. Yes.'

'Chef is not serious.'

'Chef is serious.'

'If cooking Muslim food in the kitchen is going to establish peace in the country then I am willing to convert for a day,' I said.

'*Bewakuf*,' he said. 'Idiot.'

Chef cooked Muslim Kashmiri delicacies with his own hands passionately and with great care, like a *wazwan*. Who taught him? I asked. Later, he said, I will tell you later, *you Sikh*. But he never did. For me it was a god-sent opportunity to learn the exotic cuisine, the names of Kashmiri Muslim dishes (thirty-six to be exact) unfamiliar to me, some right out of a fairy tale. I knew the Hindu Kashmiri dishes, but they were different. Certain Muslim dishes involved pounding the meat for seven or eight hours until it separated into fibres as thin as silk. We cooked in a tent pitched in the garden behind the mosque. I am still able to recall the

96

copper vessels and slow fire. I remember setting up the long dining table under the plane tree. Tarami plates. White linens fluttering in the wind.

Food was served. Fenugreek gosht. Nadir kebab. Aloobukhara korma. Goat tails. Haakh saag. Tabak maaz. Dum aloo. Rista-63. Gushtaba. Saffron pilaf in the middle. Shirmal. Rumali roti, yellow and thin like a two-day-old newspaper. No part of the tablecloth was uncovered.

They were about to start.

But.

The chief cleric asked the General to beckon the 'cook'. The cleric said: I want to have a word with the 'cook'.

Chef put on his military (jungle) hat and asked me to accompany him. I adjusted my black turban and buttoned up my white jacket. We walked together to the tree and stood before the table, silently, waiting. The colonel of the regiment, sitting on the left of General Sahib, said, 'Kishen, Pir Sahib would like to ask you a question.' The imam was sitting on the right of the General.

Chef stood confidently, just a bit ahead of me, his hands clasped behind his back.

The imam opened his mouth. I only want to double-check if the meat used in Rogan Josh is halal? he inquired.

I sighed in relief. Chef reassured the imam and the other clerics that the meat used was pure halal, but he didn't stop there. He uttered a few things, a few extra things, which I think ruined him.

This is what he said, I hear those words even now: One hundred percent halal was used, sir, we procured the meat from a genuine Muslim shop in Lal Chowk. Many interesting dishes can be prepared with pork, sir — whether it is halal or not. But we did not use pork. Only lamb was used, sir. Personally I am not for slaughtering pigs.

The situation around the table grew tense. The imam looked as if he was about to vomit.

General: Pork has not been used?

Chef: Lamb meat was used, sir.

General Sahib looked at the imams, then at the colonel of the regiment.

Colonel: No pork has been used, sir.

Chef: Only lamb was used, sir. Hundred percent halal, sir.

The imams did not touch the meat dishes. They ate very little, and hurried to the inspection tent in their dark cloaks. Some of us from the kitchen followed as well.

Our army had set up a huge shamiana tent on the uppermost terrace of the garden. The imams were seated on the carpet, and I saw the General and the police chief standing close by with burning anxiety on their faces. The vial passed from one hand to other, and eventually it ended in the hands of the holiest man, the head imam, and he sat there gazing with wonder, and it took him twenty minutes to pass his verdict, and I did not see him nod, but I saw the tense expression on the police chief's face change into a smile, and I heard the General's sigh of relief.

The vial was returned to the mosque, put in the high-security room, and the protests stopped on the streets. I did not know then that those hours were the last few hours of my apprenticeship.

The next day Chef got a written order from the colonel's office. He had been demoted, and was being transferred (with immediate effect) to the Siachen Glacier in the Karakoram mountains.

So I was now Chef.

★   ★   ★

Before he left I cooked Italian tortellini and poured him a tall glass of Kingfisher beer. During that dinner he played the slow movement of the German music on the tape recorder and told me many personal things, which to me at that moment sounded a bit comical. But with time the same things have become less and less comical. He talked about his family.

He began by telling me that the Kashmiri Hindus had no problems eating meat.

'Brahmins do not eat meat,' I protested.

'They do, Kirpal. In Kashmir the Hindus eat goat and mutton. In olden days they used to eat cows, peacocks . . . Don't give me that look.'

He poured another glass of Kingfisher.

'In this country, Kip, we have too many taboos, and sometimes I get sick of them, really sick of them.'

'But, Chef, in college the teacher told us that because of these taboos we Indians, Hindus and Sikhs and Muslims, were able to rise up against the British in 1857. The colonial officers introduced the Enfield rifle. It was bad technology, the soldiers were told to bite the cartridges in order to load the rifles. The cartridges were greased with offensive pig fat or cow fat . . . We refused. Mutiny! Our first war of independence!'

'Yes, yes,' he said. 'But that was then.'

'But it is true, Chef,' I said.

'In 1857 you Sikhs sided with the British.'

'Chef, you are trying to lump all Sikhs into one,' I said. 'As if there is only one kind of curry powder? One kind of mango? One kind of Rogan Josh?'

'One kind of woman!'

'But, Chef, I am serious.'

'So am I,' he said. 'So am I. You see, Kirpal, the foods I don't eat, the things I find disgusting, have more to do with my memories and less with religion. Take chocolate. I run away from rooms in which I sense its presence.'

'Why so?'

'Because of my father,' he said.

'Father?' I said.

'In the hospital on his deathbed my old man had desired chocolate,' said Chef Kishen. 'I hurried to the shop in the bazaar. By the time I returned he was dead. Since that moment I find the smell of chocolate repulsive. Sometimes I hear my father saying to me, Son, eat a chocolate, for my sake eat it. But the moment I see or smell it the desire gets crushed.

'But the story I really want to tell involves my grandfather,' said Chef Kishen. 'Despite being a Brahmin my grandfather didn't believe in caste. He did not believe in taboos, Kip. Grandfather rarely entered the kitchen. He was not a cook, yet he knew his food well. He didn't care who cooked in the kitchen as long as the *veg* or *non-veg* or whatever it was was good. Grandfather was married to an old woman who was a bad cook and she believed in caste. She made it very clear that she would die if a *low caste* ever cooked for her. One day the old woman was unwell and a low-caste woman took over the kitchen, and the moment grandfather revealed the identity of the cook, the old woman died. Her head fell on the bowl of curry on the table. The whole table became yellow with stains. The low-caste woman, the cook, became my grandmother.

'And yet, in the end,' said Chef, 'no matter how hard we try — we are low-caste peoples and we do not matter. Army belongs to officers, Kirpal. I am worthless. I feed them, serve them, take *ardors*. I endure the heat of the tandoor, and then I am let go, or I leave on my own. My life has come to nothing. My work has come to nothing. What will I do there on the glacier? They eat canned food on high altitudes. We are the people who do not matter. *Bleedy bastards*,' he said.

This was one of the few English words he knew. He said it in a thick accent. 'What is the meaning of 'bleedy bastards', Kip?' I told him the meaning, and he confessed that all along he had imagined it to be the equivalent of *bhaen-chod* or *ma-dar-chod*.

We are the people who do not matter, he said. Bloody bastards.

There was a single tortellini left on his

otherwise polished plate. He picked it up with his thumb and first finger.

'Kip, this thing reminds me of a woman's belly button.'

'A woman's what, sir?'

'Navel.'

'I wouldn't know, sir.'

'Here,' he said. 'Hold it.'

I held the tortellini in my left hand for a brief second and touched it with the first finger of my right, and surveyed the curious irregular shape. Then I turned it and turned it again and without hesitation put it in my mouth.

'*Congratulations*, Chef!' he said.

★　★　★

Next day Kishen took the bus to the glacier.

Two

11

So many things begin with an egg. Your tumor looks like an egg, said the doctor. Three months to a year, he said with alarming precision. Surgery might help. Chemical therapy is torture, but it might prolong your life.

Doctor, I can't afford the treatment, I told him. Just tell me what I am in for. Expect a few changes, he said. You are a cook, isn't it? Cancer is an illness that cooks the innards of the body. It spreads from organ to organ eating itself, sometimes slowly, sometimes quickly. Time will come when you will not be able to hold a spoon or a pen. You will lose feeling on one side of your face. You will lose your hair, words, memories. Time will e-vap-o-rate. Space will con-den-se. Your nose will not be able to tell the difference between kara parshad and pizza. Appetite for food and sex will wither. Just like everything else, he said, food and sex reside in the brain. You will repeat yourself. You will confuse thoughts and words. You will try to say one thing but something else will come out of your mouth. You will speak your own language like a foreigner. Foreign words and accents will roll out of your mouth. People will get the wrong impression that you are trying very hard to become an Englishman or a Yankee. You will grow angry at yourself, but you will be more angry at others. You will use lots of foul, obscene words. Galis.

He sounded like a fortune-teller.

'Shit,' I said.

'Certain things can at best be delayed. But,' he said, 'don't give up hope.'

'Does my cancer really look like . . . '

'Do not worry. Right now it is the size of a pinhead. Here.' He pointed at the CAT scan the way palmists point at lines on one's hands. Looking at that shape I felt dizzy and my head started cracking and throbbing and pounding and that was the precise moment when my transformation began, my dying.

So many things begin with an egg, I say to myself.

★ ★ ★

The train is roaring over a bridge. I feel dizzy on the window seat. India keeps passing by. The melancholy villages keep passing by. How much I like these villages, and how much I am repelled by my fellow passengers. Civilians. We are racing at an alarming speed.

The old engine is suddenly trying to make up for the lost time.

I will miss the bus to the mountains if the train fails to *cover time*.

There is one thing the doctor said which keeps coming to me. Cells, Kirpal. Our bodies, you see, are made of cells at the most *fundamental level*, he said. Cells are constantly taking birth and dying inside us. Every cell knows when to kill itself. But cancer cells refuse to do so, they keep giving birth to more and more cells, and refuse to die themselves. People with cancer die, Kirpal, because at the fundamental level their bodies start craving immortality.

On this train I feel like a man who has already expired. Unable to endure so many civilians. I don't desire to be immortal. Old passengers leave, new ones occupy the seats. They are all the same, no difference, and I am ashamed of them, all of them. The more I witness their lives the more ashamed I feel. Ashamed of my country. Is it for them my father died? Did we lose so many of our men in the army for such useless people?

Eight people on my left are speaking at the same time, they are inebriated and discussing plans to immigrate to America; another group across the aisle prefers Australia. I have decided not to speak to them at all. If I tell them about my time in the army they will say: 'We would like to hear stories about the heroism of our soldiers.' These people think war is TV.

Not far from me a man and his wife are sitting. It seems they have gone without sleep for nights. He is bald and she is on the plump side. They are a slightly older couple than the honeymooning pair I encountered last night. Not a word has been exchanged between us. But they are horrible. I had to endure them when the train stopped unexpectedly an hour ago.

When we came to a halt, the man lifted the window shutter and tapped on the wife's shoulder.

'I am stepping down,' he said.

'It is a small station,' she said.

'Forty minutes halt.'

'Who told you?'

He did not respond.

'Don't go far away.'

He wiped his shirt with his hand, and walked past other passengers, and stood by the open door. It was early in the morning, but already very hot. On the left end of the station there was a pile of dismantled army vehicles and a badly damaged MIG-21 fighter plane, with only one wing.

The platform was animated with civilians

and stray dogs and white foreigners in Indian dress. Cows were chewing on the garbage inside the bins and outside the bins. The man succeeded in making eye contact with his wife from the platform. She smiled and beckoned him towards her window.

'What station is this?' she asked loudly. He moved very close to the shutter of her window and leaned against the horizontal bars.

'There,' he said, pointing his finger. 'I can't read the sign properly.'

He stood there sweating, and a long time passed before another word was exchanged. He unbuttoned his shirt and touched his bald head.

'It is hot,' she said. 'Where is your hat?'

'I am fine. Just fine.'

The girl selling tea and pakoras stopped before the man. She looked like a gypsy. The man ordered.

The girl produced two teas in earthen cones.

'Should we get a plate of pakoras as well?' the man asked.

His wife didn't respond.

The silences were not awkward. I think this is how all married people eventually become.

The gypsy girl looked at the wife while the man transferred a cone of chai through the window. The wife returned the gaze. There were blisters on the girl's feet, red dots in the middle, and red circles around them. She wore bangles all the way from wrists to shoulders, they chimed when she lifted her arms.

'Pakoras, Memsahib?' she asked.

'No,' the wife said. 'No pakoras.'

'Egg pakoras, Memsahib.'

'No.'

'Take it, Memsahib!'

'Go away,' the wife almost screamed.

The civilian man took the plate and started eating greedily.

'Did you find out the name of the station?' the wife asked.

'Don't worry,' he said, 'this is not Pokhran.'

'Why did we have to take this train?'

'Don't start again,' he said. 'You have such a negative attitude.'

'You started it.'

'I don't understand you.'

She picked up the book she was reading and opened it randomly.

'Listen,' the man said to his wife, 'the lady-doctor says she can do it quickly. Nothing goes inside you.'

'But I don't want to get it done.'

'Don't worry. I will go with you. The lady-doctor says it is safer than X-ray.

112

Ultrasound is like taking a picture only.'

'But I really don't want to.'

'Think about it.'

His fingers were grubby with pakoras.

'For you I will do anything. But not this thing,' she said.

'Please don't do it if you feel like that. No one is forcing you.'

'What if the picture isn't right?'

'It will be all right.'

'Are you sure?'

'Have I ever lied to you?'

'But how can one be sure?'

'Because if it isn't all right then we must find out a way to fix it. Don't you want it to be all right?'

'But what if it is a girl?'

'Of course it will be a boy.'

'You don't like girls?'

'I like you,' the man said. 'I go to work every morning because I like you. Have I done anything to show I don't like you?'

'I know you like me. But would you stop liking me if I don't get this thing done?'

'You don't go to the lady-doctor, nothing will change between us. I assure you. But, it will make me unhappy.'

'What if it is a girl?'

'What can I do to make you think positive?'

'How can you be sure?'

He took a coin from his pocket. He flipped the coin thrice, using his grubby fingers.

'See,' he said. 'Three times sure. It will be a boy.'

'Stop it. I want to read my book. Just stop it.'

'Did I ever stop you?' he said and moved away from her on the platform, and beckoned the gypsy girl and ordered more tea.

The girl tried to hand him two orders, but he took only one.

'Memsahib is not having,' he said, and spat on the platform.

He slurped loudly. She put a finger in her ear. He ate two more pakoras before the guard pressed the signal.

Civilians, I say to myself. Civilians.

And India started passing by all over again. The cows, the fertile fields, the dust. India picked up speed, started pacing in straight lines and curves to the highest mountains up north. Boulders of memories started echoing. Chug. Chug. Chug. I had thought travel would liberate me from the burden of memories. When one is neither here nor there, when there is so much space and so much sky outside the window, I had imagined time would finally liberate me. But exactly the reverse is happening.

12

There are two kinds of chefs in this world. Those who disturb the universe with their cooking, and those who do not dare to do so. I am of the last kind. I try to make myself invisible. Don't get me wrong. Great satisfaction comes to me watching people praise my dishes. And yet . . . Food that draws attention to itself is not my idea of perfection.

'Bad' cooking, of course, draws attention, but so do dishes that are technically considered 'good'. The 'best' preparation is the one that transports people elsewhere, far away from the table.

Chef Kishen *dazzled* the table. I, on the other hand, transport people to *dazzling* places. But I have never been able to cook like him. His touch was precise. As if music. He appraised fruits, vegetables, meats, with astonishment, and grasped them with humility, with reverence, very carefully as if they were the most fragile objects in the world. Before cooking he would ask: Fish, what would you like to become? Basil, where did you lose your heart? Lemon: It is not *who* you touch, but *how* you touch. Learn from big elaichi. There, there. Karayla, meri jaan, why are you so prudish? . . . Cinnamon was 'hot', cumin 'cold', nutmeg caused good erections. Exactly: 32 kinds of tarkas. 'Garlic is a woman, Kip. Avocado, a man. Coconut, a hijra . . . Chilies are South American. Coffee, Arabian. 'Curry powder' is a British invention. There is no such thing as *Indian* food, Kip. But there are *Indian methods* (Punjabi-Kashmiri-Tamil-Goan-Bengali-Hyderabadi). Allow a dialogue between *our* methods and the ingredients from the rest of the world. Japan, Italy, Afghanistan. Make something new. Channa goes well with artichokes. Rajmah with brie and parsley. Don't get stuck inside nationalities.' I would watch the movement of his hands for hours on end. Once the materials stripped themselves bare, Chef mixed them with all that he remembered, and all that he had forgotten. Sometimes he would contradict himself, and that was the toughest thing to master in the kitchen.

The day I discovered I had cancer something happened to my hands. They looked exactly the same, the same shape, but I tore a chapatti a little differently, and I picked up fruits from the bowl differently, gazed at them a little longer than I used to. Even the glass of water didn't get lifted the usual way. It appeared as if time had

116

expanded and was distorting into patterns I didn't know. I felt the heat of a spoon, its coldness. I became that coldness.

★ ★ ★

Before he left by bus to the glacier, Kishen asked me to take *care* of the nurse in the hospital. How was I to take *care* of her? She had already said no to my advances, and I felt humiliated. But our next meeting was inevitable. Eight days after Chef's departure I noticed a dense fog building up outside. Standing by the window, peeling an onion, I felt an immense need to see her. It was as if a garden had grown inside me. I ordered my assistant to take over, and walked down the hill to the hospital.

Once it was a mosque and the hospital now had a green dome. It was a modest but magical-looking place. When I arrived she was busy in the ward, and asked me to wait outside in the hall.

There I waited half an hour, my gaze fixed on the floor. The black and white square tiles looked freshly mopped, not a single particle of dust on them. At last she emerged. Along came the smell of penicillin and talcum powder. Afternoon, I said. She seized my arm. A current passed through me.

'Can you visit me this evening?'

'Your home?' I asked.

She nodded.

'Right now I am in a hurry,' she said.

There was a small mole on the left side of her nose as if a seed of black cardamom. I felt like touching the mole, but there was no time. A patient cried *sister, sister*. The nurse consulted her wristwatch. Well, she said. Later, I said, and we began walking in opposite directions.

The Rogan Josh I prepared that day was one of my best. My assistant asked many questions about *origins* and *authenticity* and I found myself responding like Chef Kishen. Major, this tastes of heaven, he said. Good, I said. Now you take your break. Watching him disappear through the kitchen door I thought of a boat I had seen in the Dal Lake — it was called *heevan*. The painter had misspelled 'heaven' as 'heevan' and for a brief second I felt as if God had misspelled my fate in more or less the same way. I have a great talent to ruin things when they start shaping up. But that day, when the fog lifted, I was on top of the world, and dark thoughts could not win the tug of war. General Sahib was not supposed to eat at home in the evening. He was to dine at the Alpha Officers' Mess with commissioned officers and their wives. It was my day off. I was ready to transfer the lamb to the tiffin-carrier when Sahib's ADC made an entry, parting the curtains.

'Kip, who are you cooking the Rogan Josh for?'

'Oh,' I said cautiously, 'for tomorrow, sir.'

'Sahib prefers fresh food.'

'My mistake, sir. It will not happen again.'

Then he was unusually nice to me.

'Sahib often praises your preparations. The subzi you made a few days ago was most karari, and piyaz with fish tikka were exemplary. Shabash! Well done!' he said, and patted me on the back.

'Thank you, sir.'

'Also,' he said, 'I am very impressed you are bringing knowledge from other officers' kitchens to Gen Sahib's residence.'

'Thank you, sir.'

He was the first officer (and dancer) to have stepped in the kitchen, ever, in my presence. His rank was that of a captain.

'Kip,' he said, 'this evening the General would like to reward you and other staff members, too, for all the good work and for maintaining highest standards.'

'Sir.'

'Before the function begins this evening in the Officers' Mess, General Kumar will have rum with the entire staff on the lawns of the Mess.'

'Rum, sir?'

'Everyone must attend. Seventeen-twenty hours, sharp. Understand?'

'Yes, sir.'

'Now make me a quick nimbu-pani.'

Rum with the General on the lawns of the Officers' Mess was a rare honor for us, the staff members. I was doubly excited. But this new development cut into the time I could spend at the nurse's quarter. I did not want to hurry her. I did not want to talk about work at all, or brag about the rare honor I was about to receive from Sahib.

Evening came and I polished my shoes and took longer than usual to tie my turban in front of the mirror. I wore my blue shirt and black pants and felt slightly uncomfortable because the clothes were just like new. She lived not far from the Dal Lake. On the way to her house I kept thinking about how my body felt in my clothes. I kept delaying. At the side of the lake, I looked at the water, the waves, and for a brief moment sat on a rock and when I turned I noticed a man fishing. Salaam, he said, and I recall my response was extremely slow.

'What fish are you looking for?'

'Trout,' he said.

It occurred to me that he had been sitting there for a long time. There were no fish in his bucket. Not far from him I saw half-open blue irises and I plucked one. I had forgotten to bring along a proper gift, other than Rogan Josh and garlic naan in the tiffin carrier.

I stood before her door. The curtain was made of beads. When she appeared I did not know how to greet, so I simply apologized for being late. Then she also apologized. She too had been late. For a moment, she said, I thought you came here, and not finding me in, you left. It is not *cool* to be late, she said.

Inside, she grabbed my arm again. Sorry, she said. I am not going to offer you tea or snacks, but there is something 'you must know.'

'Please don't tell it right away,' I said. 'I already know what you are trying to say.'

She installed my flower in the vase.

Something made me wipe the crumb of bread from her kameez. Kishen treats you just like his son, she said. I nodded. It is true, I said. I agree whole-heartedly. Do you know he keeps a journal?

'Yes,' she said. 'He mentioned it to me once.'

'Not everyone knows.'

'Did you ever read it?' she asked in Hindi.

'No, but two days before he left Chef woke me up in the middle of the night. He was scribbling something. What is your best experience with food, Kip? His voice was very disturbed. I rubbed my eyes. Why wake me up at this insane hour? Tell me, he said. First you tell, I insisted. The best meal I ever had was at a dhaba in Amritsar. Me too, I lied. I don't know why I lied. The dhaba food was not even half as good as the dal-roti at the Golden Temple. His gaze settled on me for a long time before it turned absolutely cold and he started jotting again in the journal and I went back to sleep. In my dream I saw a plate and a bowl, both made out of miniature fig leaves. The leaves were stitched together with toothpicks.'

Telling her about the dream made me feel better. But her mind was elsewhere. She kept looking at the vase on the table. The dots on the vase were almost the same size as her mole. 'I want to tell you something,' she said.

'Later,' I said. 'Gen Sahib is going to honor me this evening in the Officers' Mess. How proud Kishen will be when he gets to hear it! Often I hear an echo of his voice: Cook without fear of failure, Kip. But, you must never fail.'

'I do not know how to tell you this, but I must,' she said. 'I know Kishen has not shared this with you, and that is why I must. We are not married, but we are like husband and wife.'

'You are like what?'

'Husband and wife, you know what I mean?'

'Yes, yes,' I said.

'That is why,' she said, 'it is not good when I see you giving me that look. I have sensed it in your eyes many times and I would like to tell you that it is not right.'

'I am sorry,' I said.

'No, I am sorry,' she said, 'and I have no tea to offer you.'

I did not know whether to stay or leave.

From her window that huge mass of snow and ice was faintly visible on the distant mountains, and I took a few steps to the window and looked at that thing for a long time.

What is a thing called a *glacier*? I asked myself. Layer over layer of ice. Snow from hundreds of years ago. Peel this one and then peel that one. Endless, limitless, thankless work. It cuts one's fingers. Endless, limitless, thankless work. The glacier deceived people, it didn't even reveal its actual size or intentions or the number of layers. No, it was not. The glacier was not a thing of beauty. It was one big white onion. It brought tears to one's eyes. Useless tears, I say to myself. The saddest thing about those tears was that they were absolutely useless.

She tapped on my shoulder, and when I turned she hugged me, and said: Now go.

I left the Rogan Josh next to the vase on the table. Under the table there were three miniature battle tanks. They glared at me. I'd not noticed them earlier. Centurions: manufactured in England. Now go, she insisted. Without a proper namasté I stepped out towards the Officers' Block. It was getting dark and chilly and I passed lots of jeeps and black cars parked on both sides of the road. I made it exactly twenty minutes before rum at the Alpha Officers' Mess.

The Mess was bright both inside and outside. The lawn was lit up with floodlights. The flowers that lined the lawn were red and yellow and purple, and they were the size of footballs. We lined up outside on the lawn. The gardener Agha, the water carrier, the sweeper, the orderlies — the entire staff that worked at Sahib's residence.

There were two empty chairs on the lawn, and behind those chairs the little girl Rubiya appeared: 'Daddy, the men are here!'

But as soon as she said that the girl ran away as if afraid of us.

Then all of a sudden I heard confident footsteps pounding on the pebbled path. General Sahib stepped out in his dashing civilian clothes, wearing an impressive tie. He walked up close to the line, shaking our hands one by one.

'Stand at ease,' said the colonel of the regiment.

It was the second time I stood next to General Sahib face to face, and I did not know how to conduct myself in front of him. I stood to attention the way my father used to in the photos. The General looked at me with piercing eyes.

'The army is proud of your father.'

'Sir.'

He patted my back.

'You know, Kirpal, Major Iqbal did all the work and I got the baton.'

I did not know what to make of it.

Then the General laughed.

I still recall the fine cut of his dark blue jacket and the red and blue regimental tie. Sahib was around forty-nine then, that day we had rum, and he did not change much as long as I knew him. I remember he had a large collection of ties. The width of his ties changed according to the fashion of the year. Narrow. Broad. Narrow again. His neck was long and his face sharp and clean-shaven.

'We are impressed by your exemplary work,' he said.

'Thank you, sir.'

'The colonel has recommended you for a

promotion, Kirpal.'

'Sir.'

'Now you are only one rank short of an officer.'

'Thank you, sir.'

'Let us drink to that.'

We clinked our rum glasses. I looked at General Sahib in the eye.

'You are very handsome, my boy,' said the General.

'Thank you, sir.'

'Beautiful. Just like a woman, sir,' said the ADC from far away.

'Are you happy?' said the General.

'Sir, is it possible to go on a three-day casual leave, sir?'

'When?'

'First week of July, sir.'

'Delhi?'

'No, sir. Glacier, sir.'

'I understand, Kirpal. Your father . . . '

Then he turned to the colonel: 'Send Kip on some duty to the glacier. Is there a vehicle going?'

'I will look into that, sir. But, for now the situation is unstable.'

The General turned and saw Colonel Chowdhry's wife enter the Officers' Mess. The other officers' wives were already inside the dance hall, waiting. Particles of talcum powder kept floating towards us on the lawn. The light in that room was faint and weak and before the colonel's wife stepped inside she smiled at me from a distance.

'What is going on?' exclaimed the General. '*Pakistan* is inside, and *India* is outside! This is unfair!'

The officers laughed. Loud music could be heard.

'Very unfair, sir. The gentlemen are outside, and the ladies are inside.'

'Unfair,' repeated the General.

'Start the party, sir?'

'Yes. Yes,' he said to them.

'Jai Hind,' he said to us.

'Jai Hind, sir.' We clicked our heels.

The General saluted and hurried towards the dance hall. Other ranks followed him.

I returned to my room after a long walk along the river. Only once I felt the need to splash my face with water. It was ice cold.

13

If you want something, my mother had told me when I was a boy, you say no and then say no again and the third time you say *Okay, a little*. She was talking about food when it is offered at some other person's house. Our guests had offered us the betel leaf cone, and I said no, then no again, and I was ready to say *Okay, a little* but the hosts didn't offer the paan the third time. At home I screamed at the top of my voice. I want that betel nut thing now, right now. Neighbors gathered around our house, probed my parents why they were torturing me. Next time you want something, said my father, grab it.

The nurse, I just learned, was not up for grabs. Memsahib was, but I was afraid of her, and of the colonel. I was afraid of losing my fingers. Ideally, I wanted to become a vegetable. The vegetables were not afraid of anything. *The carrots were fucking the earth.* The carrots and onions were having better sex than me. Zucchini made scandalous love to paneer, mushrooms, garlic and tomatoes. Basil coated the deep interiors of fully swollen pasta, with names sexier than shapes.

R-i-g-a-t-o-n-i! F-u-s-i-l-l-i! C-o-n-c-h-i-g-l-i-e! Gulmarg salad licked walnut chutney in public. Even brinjal (that humble eggplant), swimming in a pot of morkozhambu, insisted on having more pleasure than me.

Patience, Kip.

How impatient we people are in this country. Yet how patient we are when it comes to food. We wait for a long time to get it right, I say to myself on the window seat. I wanted to speed things up, force them into bending my way, and the result was a disaster. I seem to have no talent for forcing things my way.

I stopped using the cycle. I would go to the bazaar to buy vegetables on military transport. Sometimes when the curfew was in place the ADC would arrange a jeep. One morning I found that the General's staff car was taking the black dog to the vet, and I requested the driver to give me a lift. The dog was in great pain, eyes running. Sitting in the car, I found it difficult to endure the animal's whine. What is it? I asked. The orderly and the driver did not know for sure. No idea, Major. Just doing our duty, Major. The dog stank of a strange disease.

They dropped me in the bazaar, and took the road to the vet's clinic. The bazaar was crowded and dusty and noisy as usual. Sad

129

and miserable people milled around in colorful robes. I bought fresh herbs and fish and vegetables and fruit. For several hours I waited in the street, elbow to elbow, but the car did not return. Fortunately, there was a military transport parked close by, and the driver, an acquaintance of mine, gave me a lift.

On the way just outside the Mughal garden the nurse was standing at the bus stop. The driver slowed down.

'I am in a hurry,' I said.

He stopped not far from her and honked.

'Going to the army camp?'

She nodded.

'Get in,' he said.

She squeezed in beside me and lit up a cigarette as soon as she settled.

'Please don't smoke in the truck,' I said.

'It is OK, *Major*,' said the driver, smiling at us in the mirror. 'Let her.'

She made brief eye contact with me, then threw the cigarette out the window. The shopping bags were squeezed in the space between our legs. I picked up the strawberries, which were wrapped in an old English newspaper. The color red had wicked into the yellow of the paper, the Government was planning to construct a railway track all the way to Kashmir. I sliced the strawberries with my army knife. I am not hungry, she said. Take some home, I suggested. I don't like cherries and strawberries, she muttered and sat there silently. Just before the driver made it to the camp gates we heard sounds of sirens. Emergency vehicles were heading downtown. He turned around and stopped not far from the hospital. Without saying a word, she jumped out of the truck.

The truck would not start up right away. From the window I watched as she opened her purse and dug out a fresh cigarette and put it between her lips. Camel. It was an imported Camel. Her hands started searching for a light. There was a matchbox in the driver's shirt. He gave it to me and I jumped out and ran to her and struck a light. She turned away. I struck another, but again she turned her head.

'Why don't you just give it to her,' yelled the driver.

'OK,' I said.

She struck the match herself.

'This is my last cigarette,' she said before disappearing.

*　*　*

In the kitchen I heard that the General's car had been grenade-attacked downtown. The

131

news terrified me. *Kashmiris*, Major. *Terrorists*, Major. Close to the vet's clinic the car had slowed down to negotiate the speed-breaker when a Kashmiri lobbed a grenade. The car shot up in the air and was ripped to pieces. Although the driver and the orderly had escaped unharmed the dog had been badly wounded.

General Sir rushed to the site with his staff members and a curfew was imposed on the city. Sirens echoed in the valley.

The ADC was in a bad mood when he marched into the kitchen to inform me that Sahib was going to skip the Sandhurst curry that night. No dinner for Rubiya either, he added. The girl is very sad. There is no point cooking the dinner.

'But how can you be sure, sir?'

'As I say.'

'But, sir, during times like these one feels more hungry, not less.'

'As I say.'

'Sir.'

'General Sir will drink coffee only,' he said. 'And you, Kirpal, will take the tray to his room. Twenty-one hundred hours. Sharp.'

'Me, sir?'

'Your day has come. Tonight you will serve Sahib in his room. Understand?'

'Sir.'

'And do not forget the hot-water bottle.'

'Yessir.'

I was nervous and ran to my room and shared the news with my assistant. He was busy looking at porn magazines.

'Major,' he cried loudly, 'girls are heaven.'

I told him that touching oneself makes one weak. Touching oneself was not real. He seemed to disagree with me.

'Major, look at her momays!'

He had a pile of *Debonairs* and *Playboys* on his bed.

It used to be my bed. But after Chef was posted to the glacier, I moved to his bed, and the assistant occupied my old bed.

'Masturbation is bad,' I said.

'Major, what is wrong with making love to oneself? If one can cook for oneself, then one can also touch oneself.'

'It is not *real*.'

'Major, have you ever seen a naked girl before? Come. Here. Look. *Nangi Ladki*.'

A helpless rage filled me. Anger began flowing inside me, and the tray shook as if the earth was shaking when I marched to Sahib's room. I was wearing Sahib's old clothes and shoes, which I had received on Diwali day, and I stood outside his room at twenty-one hundred hours, sharp.

I froze in my position, waited outside

longer than I should have. I could not believe what I heard. I think inside the room he was weeping. Sahib was listening to some soft ghazal music, the notes were extremely melancholic. But he was weeping as well. He was very attached to the dog and he was weeping. I stood outside for a long time with milk, coffee, sugar, cups, and silver spoons, and finally when my courage returned I tapped twice or thrice on the door. But the taps must have been very, very light, they must have felt like the passing breeze to the General inside that room. I tiptoed to the kitchen, transferred the coffee to a thermos, and left the tray outside the door by the mat. Then I returned to my room.

My assistant was still up on his bed, on his elbows, looking at the glossy magazines. He reeked of rum. The room had the odor of sperm. There is no privacy in the army unless one is an officer. That was the first time I lost my patience. I yelled at him. Touching oneself is not *real*, I repeated. Shut the light and go to bed, I said. That night I listened to special music. Chef had given me a cassette of German music as a parting gift. The music went fast, then slow, fast, slow and fast again. Listening to those beautiful foreign sounds made me forget where I was and made me forget about masturbation.

The dog never returned to its old self again. It had lost an eye, and the vision in the other eye already had grown very dim. So it would circle round and round. There was hardly any flesh left on its hind legs. Little Rubiya thought that the dog loved moving in spiraling circles and semicircles. She would count the circles like an expert mathematician. Zero. One. Two. Three.

Kip-ing!

Sometimes Rubiya, trying to catch butterflies, would drift towards my quarter, but the ayah would come after her. The girl hated school and would often try to run away. She flared her nostrils while telling me about another then another escape from school. The girl's face resembled the dead woman in the painting, but her eyes were different, tiny, her legs thinner than lotus roots. Her cheeks were soft but dry, I knew this even without touching them.

Rubiya and I, even then, despite her ayah, developed a special understanding, which goes beyond words. Sometimes when Sahib happened to be a little annoyed with my performance, Rubiya would wink or smile or give me a look which meant I understand, don't worry, my father is a bit out of his mind. He is a bit fussy, that is all.

How could I have predicted then that she

was going to become someone big one day? How could I have seen the poet in Rubiya?

Those days there was dust in my eyes, but let me say it again, those days were really the golden age in Kashmir.

14

The reason the enemy was able to cross the border and set up their camp on the glacier is because our Intelligence officers were sleeping, or playing golf, or building hotels and gyms and malls in Delhi, or they were drinking rum. And polishing their American accents. The enemy knew this and meanwhile entered the country and built bunkers high up on the mountains. Mules and helicopters had transferred rations to the bunkers, and our Intelligence officers kept sleeping. Our leaders kept posing for the Lahore-Delhi bus diplomacy photos, and no one knew that General Musharraf and members of his staff had crossed the Line of Control to visit the so-called freedom fighters, the soldiers of the Pakistani 5th Light Infantry, who had built concrete bunkers in our land. By the time the local villagers informed our army about the infiltrators it was too late. Thousands of enemy guns and men had crossed into our territory, and our men started dying like sheep and dogs.

Early in June news reached us in the kitchen that the situation had shifted from bad to worse in the border areas of Kargil, eighteen thousand feet high. My assistant had to leave the kitchen on a convoy to the front, and he died in Tololing. Time flowed differently now for us in the kitchen — breakfast was served at night and lunch at five in the morning and dinner at noon. On certain days all we managed to whip up was raw and half cooked or yesterday's leftovers and many a times Sahib ate with soldiers at the border posts. During war the difference between jawans and officers diminishes, Chef used to say. They eat from the same ration.

I had lost all contact with Chef. Before the war, the radio operator Nair used to help me keep in touch with Kishen. But during the war he heard nothing from Siachen. News about him reached the kitchen only after the ceasefire, which took place sixty days later. The news was not good. He was alive. But during a two-day leave in Srinagar he had tried to kill himself.

From the kitchen window I saw helicopters hovering over the hospital and the parade ground in the valley below. They shook the plane trees left and right. I cycled to the hospital. Men dead and near dead were being whisked into Emergency. I remember the shadows of the men who carried the stretchers. Voices of soldiers who wanted to delay their amputations, the surgery, because they were hungry. They had not eaten for days.

Even the nurses and doctors looked sleep-starved and hungry. The wards were filled with dying men, and the corridors packed with badly wounded men or those with one arm or leg.

Kishen's bed was in a small room in that overflowing hospital. Normally it was a maternity room, but it had been opened up for this special 'suicide' case. The matter was under investigation. Two guards stood outside the room. Kishen, glacier-wallah, is in operating theatre, they told me. When will he return? We don't know. We know nothing. No one knew what was going on in the hospital. There were many new nurses, and they all looked alike. I waited for a long time by the metal bed. The pillow on the bed had a hollow and I looked at the hollow and his name and rank and 23rd Battalion on a sheet glued on to the wall. His boots were under the bed. The stencil on his black trunk said: Brij Kishen, NCO, 23rd Battalion. They had moved all his things from the glacier to the ward. Lying on top of the trunk was his pen. I picked it up. I had seen him jotting in his journal with that pen many times in the kitchen.

During the war we all did unnatural things and I was no exception. Rubiya, too, those days began doing unnatural things. School was canceled. General Sahib had postponed the Goan ayah's annual leave — as a result the woman was always in a foul mood, not really taking care of the girl. Rubiya developed a fascination for observing fire. She would throw things she liked or disliked into the fireplace in the living room and watch them burn. Flames would consume the objects, soon they would crackle along the logs of pine and deodar in the fireplace, and it was possible to see the soot particles floating in the air. The girl made no distinction between what was useless and what was precious, she whimsically discarded her father's things, even her dead mother's clothes and ornaments and photos. She would sit next to the fireplace after the act and watch the roaring flames reduce the materials to ashes. She would feel the waves of heat hit her cheeks (I thought), then run away and hide for long hours somewhere in the big residence. Once or twice she was found hiding in my room, which was not even attached to the house. Several times Sahib scolded and even punished her but the war sent him away from the residence. I saw him briefly in the hospital the day I went down looking for Kishen. Back in the residence I was a bit stunned to encounter him again after such a short duration of time. Rubiya received a harsh scolding from her father during dinner. The girl refused to touch the food I had cooked and ran to her room. Sahib retired to his bedroom, he made no attempt to make up with the sobbing girl. Because of shortage of staff I doubled as the orderly and personally took the after-dinner tea to his room. He was pacing up and down in the room, which was huge, but in extreme chaos, the bed unmade, the chairs and tables pointing in different directions. I left the tray on the center table. On the side of the table I noticed a pile of confidential files and not far from the files a red journal. On the spine Kishen's Hindi signature was visible. What was it doing in Sahib's bedroom? The Hindi was a bit faded, but it was still there. I felt like flipping through it, but restrained myself.

'Kip, no need to stir sugar.'

'Sir.'

'You may leave.'

'Goodnight, sir.'

Back in the kitchen I tried to conjure up the course of events that must have happened. The CO of the regiment must have sifted through Kishen's belongings after the suicide attempt, then handed the journal to the Intelligence Branch and the intelligence-wallahs dispatched it to Gen Sahib via a senior officer.

Standing in Sahib's room I kept hearing an echo of Chef Kishen's voice. I had to do something. I was afraid, but I had to do something. 'If you see this journal in the wrong place, destroy it, Kirpal.'

This is the detail. Two days later the journal has still not left Sahib's table. I enter Sahib's room in the afternoon after his departure. I am about to pick up the thing when I hear voices. Ayah and Rubiya in the corridor. What if they discover me in the room? But. The voices recede. Soon ayah is in the bathroom, Rubiya starts playing barefoot in the garden with her dog. I am still in Gen Sahib's bedroom, standing by the table. I pick up the confidential files and the journal, rush to the warm living room.

That evening the General based on the report from ayah scolds and punishes Rubiya for having burned to ashes his important documents. That's the limit, he says. You've burned my top-secret documents. She cries. She protests. But, Papa, she says, I didn't do it. Papa doesn't believe her. Ayah doesn't believe her either. Sahib, here is the only half-burned page from those files, says the ayah. The page flew out of the fireplace, says the ayah. Papa, I didn't do it. No, Papa. The girl is losing her faith in the world. I didn't realize this thing then; now I know better.

I have never been able to pardon myself for having given the girl so many tears, so much anguish. Ever since that moment I have felt a different person. Again and again I go back to that moment. I see myself rushing to the living room with the files and the journal in my hand. Through the window I make sure Rubiya is playing in the garden outside, her dog is panting, going round in circles. I make sure I hear the sound of water in the bathroom, a woman is taking her bath in there. I am in front of the fireplace. Waves of heat hit my face. I shake, I hesitate, I sense the presence of the dead woman in the painting, her ghostly gaze. I change my mind. But my mind is made up. I let the things in my hands go. Little tongues of fire start licking the pages. Then the crackle, the sparks, the roar.

The only item I could not throw into the flames was the journal. Later in my room I opened the journal, not to judge anyone, but to simply find out why Kishen wanted to kill himself. What kind of information, scribbled inside the journal, was sensitive enough to cause its relocation to Sahib's room?

It is a little thing — seven inches by five inches — no more than two hundred pages. In Delhi, for a long time, I kept it under lock and key, but as I was setting out on this journey I picked it up and brought it with me. It is now with me on this train. The first time I tried to read it (in the General's kitchen) was extremely difficult. Chef wrote the entries very tightly, in bad handwriting, and in two languages, Hindi and Punjabi.

The first few pages are recipes of simple salads — somewhat exotic, but perfectly suitable for Indian taste buds:

Tomato and Feta Cheese Salad
900g tomatoes
200g feta cheese
120ml olive oil
12 black olives
freshly ground pepper
Serves 4

In bold letters he emphasizes: Black olives are a must, not green, not sun-dried black olives, but juicy black olives.

The next few pages are filled with complaints about the absence of olives in Indian cooking. How hard it is to find this thing in Indian stores, and the troubles he had to go through to acquire olives. He ends a page with an invention of a new olive side dish, the olive raita. He ends the next page with another invention: mirchi (green cayenne pepper) chocolate fondue. Two pages later he comments on his fascination for cheese. He complains about the lack of good cheese in Indian cooking. Paneer is fine, but there are more than 462 types of cheeses, maybe more. He praises Brie and Roquefort in particular. Why do we borrow certain things from foreigners and not the rest? he writes. Why do we adapt to tomatoes and kidney beans and not cheese? Indian cooking seems impossible without tomatoes. But tomatoes moved to our country from Mexico. Only one hundred years ago we started using them in our food. Now it is commonplace.

The French embassy-wallahs told me about a master chef, Batel or Patel his name was, and this man killed himself because he could not deliver the perfect meal. I bow before the master. I can never bring myself to do that.

Right in the middle of the journal, he talks more about his apprenticeship at five-star hotels and foreign embassies in Delhi. Of all the embassies, he received his warmest welcome from the German embassy. He writes about Chef Muller. Chef Muller introduced him not only to German cuisine, but also to music. This music I listen to when I am alone, he writes. In the kitchen I hear this music when cooking. I cannot thank Chef Muller enough for gifting me two tapes of such fine music. But, how uninteresting German cuisine is! Even the curried sausage. It is hard to comprehend how such a culture managed to produce such incredible music!

Chef's life and work are fused together; it is difficult to separate them at least in the notebook. I had expected to see more sketches. But there are only three dirty pictures. A naked woman is shoving a Cadbury's chocolate bar inside her sex. A man is balancing an orange on his erect lingam. His penis is coated with 'kamasutra powder' — the recipe is scribbled on the margin. Otherwise the pages look surprisingly clean. Only five or six have grease on them.

Flipping through, it seems as if this is my journal. I have never kept a diary, but I might have written more or less the same words. I would have skipped the dirty sex parts, but I might have written about other things in a similar way. When I read these pages I sense a remarkable similarity in voice. He was my second self or perhaps I am what he was becoming. The greatest gift he gave me was not food. Not even the foreign cuisines.

Chef gave me a tongue.

The tone changes the moment he is transferred to the glacier. But again he is talking about his plans to install the first tandoor on Siachen. He plans to use mules as transport to take the component parts to the camp on the Icefields. He proposes a detailed method on how to reassemble the parts. He does not recommend parachuting the fully assembled clay oven down on the Icefields using a helicopter. (This method was used to transfer the Swedish guns.) He uses the words 'glacier' and 'icefields' interchangeably.

In the beginning of June, he writes, with a heavy heart I quickly collected my things and left the base headquarters. We followed the long and dangerous road to Ladakh. Then a Cheetah helicopter flew us to the Icefields, a camp twenty thousand feet high. In the helicopter I was feeling dizzy. When I looked down I experienced vertigo. This was the first time I saw the Icefields from so close. They are like their name: huge white endless fields, where a hundred thousand people can play cricket and hockey for days on end. But the place is absolutely empty. Empty and desolate. Other than two little army camps there is nothing. Our camp is at a higher elevation than our enemy's.

Minus 58. God help us all.

A soldier told me that this place is the second coldest on Earth, he writes. The glacier is eighty miles long. The name means 'wild rose'. Wild roses grow at the base of this beast or organism or whatever it is. The Balti people live there, and in their language Siachen means wild rose.

Not a single day goes by without firing by either side. We never attack on Fridays. A soldier told me that Fridays privilege the enemy because it is the day of their prayer. Saturdays are better. On Saturdays the peaks flash like the inside of a tandoor.

Most of the mountain peaks here do not have names. So we give them names. Because we do not have much to do in the kitchen we find ways to amuse ourselves. Giving the peaks names kills time very well. Sometimes we give names which are abuses in our language: Ma-chod, bahenchod, bhon-sadi-day. We call our enemies Pakis or sulahs. They call us Hindu cunts. Those ma-chods, behn-chods, bhon-sadi-days. Mother fuckers. Sister fuckers.

Our homes are white arctic tents, each one with space for three sleeping bags. Evening, morning and afternoon I hear the same thing from the men: Arrange my transfer, or I am very unhappy here. Men become extremely religious here. The soldiers read Hanuman

Chaleesa and Gita if they are Hindus and Japuji if they are Sikhs, and Koran if they are Muslims, but there are not many Muslims in the army.

There are soldiers who look at photos of Bombay actresses like Shilpa Shetty (and vamps like Helen) for hours while others listen to songs on transistor radio. Some engage in thirty-second open-air pissing and spitting contests. Fluids freeze before hitting white ground. I have my Sony tape recorder here. Sometimes when I need to be alone I put on my parka and underpants under pure wool fatigues, and lace my Swiss snow boots and put on my gloves and baklava and black goggles and step out for a walk in loose, deep snow. I take my Sony along, and when I am far enough away from our camp I play Chef Muller's German music. The music is foreign to my ears and perhaps that is why I like it more than our own.

We wash once a month. We use kerosene oil to melt ice. Kerosene stoves run twenty-four hours in the tents. We have learned not to waste even a single drop of water . . . Kerosene blackens our faces, our fingers. We step out for the *call of nature*. We shit on the Icefields. The doctor has instructed us not to expose ourselves longer than thirty seconds. It is so cold on Siachen.

There is something wrong with the way we eat here. Precooked food. Canned curry and subzis. Canned rice. Chappati is a luxury. Unhealthy Maggie instant noodles. No Balti chicken. Mango frooti juice in tetrapacks. Salted Amul cheese. Butter. White bread. Cadbury chocolate bars are not for eating; we unwrap the bars and break them and dump them on the ice floor in our tents; chocolate makes ice less slippery, allowing us to walk without falling; we step on *chocolate burfi*, literally. I hate chocolate. Rum is free-flowing. Rum, too, allows us to walk. Sometimes jawans steal kebabs from the plates, which are sent to the officers' tent. I approve of this wholeheartedly.

Mustard oil is our savior. It doesn't freeze.

The Sikh soldiers experience more pain than the rest of us, he writes. Sharp crystals and icicles form in their beards. Long hair inside their turbans becomes matted automatically. They cry in pain trying to comb the hair. Halat khasta, they cry. Kip would have been dead by now.

Don't believe if someone tells you that men on the Icefields die like animals. No, they do not die like that. A mule when it slips into a crevasse cries out of agony for one full hour before slipping into deep silence. Men die either instantaneously, or take several days.

150

On 4 March Naik Surendran died in his sleep due to HAPO. Two days later a second-lieutenant fell from a height of 14,000 feet. The rescue team failed to retrieve his body. They returned with a dead corporal, the soldier's fingers stitched to his pubic hair.

There are a few breaks in the entries after this point. Two or three pages later he starts repeating himself. As if he is stuck inside a cold white vortex. Armies are supposed to be mobile tigers and foxes, he writes. But we have become ice.

Everything is white here, even time has turned white. These are my white hours. This Icefield is not for the weak-hearted. We are being killed not only by the Pakistanis but also by bitter cold. It is so cold here it eats one's brain and belly and freezes the heart. Men use jerry cans of kerosene oil to thaw the Bofors guns. We are lucky we have the Swedish Bofors guns. They can lob the forty-kilo shells (which look like jackfruit) into the enemy positions thirty or forty miles away. The guns are helping us sheeshkebab the Pakis. But to use the guns one must stand out in the cold. Men complain about mountain sickness, this condition is called HACO — a human brain drowns in its own fluids, a human body turns blue, and HAPO — a lung fails due to lack of oxygen. Men can't sleep. We hallucinate. Some hear the cries of djinns. Men become impotent. Yesterday a gunner while eating his meal broke down. He was telling us about his victories with women, and then suddenly he broke down and started weeping and said he can no longer get *it* up. It seems to me the reason he lost his manhood is because he stayed too long at this altitude. Six months without a break on Siachen. His officer could not find a replacement. I tried to console him, but he punched me in the mouth and said — what do you kitchen people know?

I did not know how to respond to this man. He was not very young, in his late twenties perhaps. The moment he broke down all the laughter in the tent ceased, and people stopped eating, and we were no longer able to talk about the red-light district of Bombay: about Kamathipoora, where Pal and Thapa had picked up gonorrhea (at first they feared it was HIV), and where Inder had slept with the impotent ship captain's pretty wife.

Flipping through these pages, I say to myself on the window seat of this train, this does not seem like the journal of a man about to kill himself or about to make a serious attempt. In the journal he writes that he admires officers who simply look the other way when men do not follow their orders on the glacier. Siachen is a strange place, he concludes. Bonds between men grow strong here, and they grow very weak, and get blown away by cold winds. If I can admire or pretend to admire the beauty of this icy wasteland, and find poetry in the tents and igloos and seracs and pinnacles and icicles, and the black soot on the walls of the igloos because of kerosene oil bukharis and braziers, and parachutes dropping parts of Bofors guns, and canned food and sheep, if I can admire all these things . . .

Then suddenly Chef writes about me. It was the second time I found myself written about.

I do not think the boy Kirpal will stay for long. He does not really belong in the army. Kip is fixated on his father. That is why he is in the army. The boy has a sensitive sense of smell — almost like a dog. One day he will sniff out the truth.

One day he will learn that to live properly, one must allow one's parents to die. Once I saw his father kiss a Kashmiri woman in the Mughal garden. I was on the other side of the fountain — they could not see me. The woman's face was wet from the mist, she spread a calico sheet on the grass under the plane tree, she sat at the edge of the sheet, hands dangling on her raised knees, she fussed about the embroidered dupatta on her

153

head, tucked neatly behind her ears and falling on both sides of her blue kameez. It was then he took the woman in his arms and turned around to check if someone was watching and once convinced that no one was close by he kissed her. It was brief, but it was definitely a kiss. She pushed him away as if trying to tell him not to take such liberties again, but really she wanted him to do exactly the opposite.

Kirpal's father belonged to the tradition of officers who were gentlemen. Officers like Maj. Gen. Khanolkar and Maj. Gen. Thimayya, Gen. Harbaksh Singh and Gen. J.S. Aurora. They knew duty, honor, humanity. Officers like him (despite the fact that they succumbed to women during weak moments) are the main reason I am still in the army. Some of our commanders here on the glacier are extremely abusive. They make this hell a bigger hell.

There are no trees here, Chef writes. One day I saw a tree and started walking towards it. But a soldier told me that it was three days away. The captain said that the tree did not exist at all. 'Go to the CO's tent if you want to see the real thing. Smaller than the size of your prick, *a Japanese bonsai*.'

Yesterday I saw a djinn, he writes a week later. He was on a serac, smoking a cigarette.

154

Save me, the djinn cried. I found it difficult to bear his agony. Save me, he screamed. Have you people forgotten how to scream? he asked. Stop it, I said. Stop smoking that bleedy cigarette, I said. Go away, you dwarf. You Ma-chod. Bhaen-chod. Bhon-sadi-day.

This journal has a burnt smell. But.

Flipping through these pages I begin to feel very cold. I am trying to find the precise page, the one I had discovered in the General's residence, the one which had given me a hint as to why Chef had tried to kill himself:

The soldiers take care of their clothes and bodies. How obedient and patient they are. When they die on duty they bring to their lips the name of their wife or simply 'O my mother'. I have heard from other soldiers. There are always some who do not return. I cook thinking they will all return. There is always someone who does not. It is hard to throw away the food. At night I hear the missing soldiers' cries: I am hungry, feed me. There is always a soldier who does not return. Sometimes to forget this hell I recite the comical names of our border posts: Khalsa 1, Khalsa 2, Romeo 1, Romeo 2. I close my eyes and recall all the street names and areas in Srinagar, where our base camp is. Habakadal. Brazulla. Jawahar Nagar. Pantha Chowk. Ganderbal. Raina Wari. Raj

Bagh. Badami Bagh. The moment I do so I see the faces of *real* people, and I am able to endure this hell. Sometimes I hear the whistle of a train approaching. It stops at a platform on the mountains. Kirpal is headed to the Badami Bagh camp. I touch the face of Kip, the boy is standing outside the General's residence. There is a tenderness in his look. Sometimes I walk by the tents at night and I feel as if we are a wrecked ship, and feel the glacier moving under my feet. Mocking me. My God, where am I?

We are condemned. For us there is no hope. The Pakistanis fire at us from the other side. Are they filled with hope? They are on lower ground than us and yet filled with hope. They believe they will go straight to heaven after they die. When we capture an enemy prisoner I cannot wait to ask him. Tell me, what does your heaven look like? Here, please draw it on this sheet of paper. What food do people eat in heaven?

Everything looks strange, he writes near the end of the journal. The war is over. I am no longer on the Icefields. Back at the base headquarters things make no sense. Men polishing officers' boots, men playing the brass band, bagpipes, the band master's baton going up in the air, parade ground, signal center, MT workshop, men playing volleyball, dry canteen and wet canteen, burra-khana and chota-khana, burra-peg and chota-peg, recreation room — nothing makes sense.

The entries from this point are written very very tightly and it is difficult to read them. They are a strange mixture of two-thirds Hindi and one-third Punjabi. His Hindi is superior to his Punjabi.

She cooks me a meal, he writes. The nurse. And while she lays the table I ask — Why do we cling to the Rose Glacier, and why does Rose cling to us?

She does not hear me. While she serves food I begin thinking about the garbage on the glacier. Our shit on the Icefields. Acres of wrecked Bofors guns and American and British weapons. Wrecked vehicles, tanks, jerry cans. What is the name of the wind that blows on the glacier? I would like to know the name of the wind.

Why are you not paying attention to me? she asks. The nurse kisses me. She undoes her blouse. Her breasts fall. I say, I thought you wanted to do it after the meal. She is somewhere behind me now. I see her petticoat string dangling from the empty chair. I turn. My heart is beating fast, fluids are running inside fast. I have not seen a woman's belly button for an entire six

157

months. I eat her tortellini. I lick her tattoo. But I am not able to get my *thing* up. In the past I would have had her before the blouse and petticoat came off. This time minutes pass and become hours. I am not able to get my thing up. I am not able to get *it* up.

She removes her three bangles and her wristwatch. Places them on the side table. Now she is completely naked and is panting like a dog and this arouses me but my thing does not harden. It does not. It is the tail of a dog. Wags a little. Only a little.

She tells me to talk to the doctor. She is a nurse. She knows these things. The next day I sit outside the doctor's door. But when my turn comes after a long wait I am unable to tell him my problem. Words remain frozen in my mouth. Instead I tell him I feel weak, very weak. He gives me Vitamin C.

For half a day I run along the river, I do not return to the nurse's quarters, I bike to the houseboat *Texas Dawn* in the red-light district to do it with a paid woman. The girl I choose is fair and sexy and well-endowed. Her name is Azra or Asma. But. The thing does not work.

The thing is wrecked.

A few pages later the address of Chef's wife in Delhi is written. There are a couple more blank pages.

Three

15

The river is brown and muddy and holy. The train roars over the bridge. The waters are sparkling with industrial froth. Naked children jump into the river. India, God's naked country, is passing by. Mustard fields sway in the wind, they are the braids of air. Waves of tractors and bullock carts. (The fields make me think about yesterday's news: mass suicides by starving farmers in the South.) Chimney smoke rises from an oil refinery. The smoke will blacken the white marble of the Taj. A pesticide factory flashes by. (The farmers killed themselves by drinking eight liters of agricultural pesticide.) Garbage. Streams of plastic. Hills of bottles, bags, wrappers. Cows chew on the plastic. Cell-phone towers. A cloud of butterflies, a little girl in a wrinkled pink frock is trying to catch them. A uranium mine. A huge banyan tree, the size of a village. Roots and knots everywhere. Nothing grows under a tree so thick. Thin dogs on a street. Fat goats. A butcher shop, condensation on the window. A temple, the gods are dancing. A ruined mosque. A herd of water buffaloes. Diseased mosquitoes hover on them. A mall building under construction. Water tanks. A receding platform, a receding city. A wave of nano cars. Then nothing. Only a profusion of signs. STD. BITS. ISD. HIV. C-h-i-l-d Beer. B-r-a-c-k-f-a-s-t. OK-TATA. 502 Bidi. Gandhi Spinal Hospital. FICCI welcomes the American President. Eat Cricket, Sleep Cricket, Drink only Coke. Veg-Non-Veg.

M-a-c B-u-g-e-r-s. D-o-m-i-n-o-s. L-a-t-i-n (not 'latrine').

God help us.

★   ★   ★

In Kashmir in autumn there are leaves which turn yellow but don't fall. They cling hard to trees. The plane leaves fall, but there are trees (whose names I do not recall now) with yellow leaves that cling to branches. Last year's leaves cling to this year's tree. Even the strongest wind cannot separate them. What force bonds them tight?

When young I used to think if I picked up a terminal disease I would kill myself. But now my ideas on this have changed. I would like to cling to whatever life is left within me.

But.

There is one thing he wrote in the journal that burns me, and no matter how hard I try

162

to forget, the thing still burns me. If someone else had said such things about me, I would not have given it much importance, but Kishen wrote those things with his own hand. That is why I was angry. I was angry at him and angry at myself for not expressing my anger. Despite his words I continued feeding him in the hospital while he was convalescing. I never brought it up.

I am reading the journal again and my hands shake.

Chef's allegation involves General Sahib.

The other day I was sitting with a soldier in the hospital canteen, he writes, and the soldier uttered something vulgar about the nurse. She is a cockteaser, he said. She has a tattoo on her belly. I grabbed him by the collar. She is mine, I said. Leave her alone. Are you sure she is yours, Major? the soldier asked. She only *does it* with the officers. The soldier's remark fumed me, increased my anger, he writes. How do you know she has a tattoo on her belly when she only *does it* with the officers? When you were away to the glacier, Major, she went to the border post with General Kumar and they spent the night in the same bunker. Two months later Sahib sent her to the Delhi HQ hospital for a while. The staff in Delhi told us that the rose tattoo had become a grotesque-shaped flower when her belly had swollen, and even more grotesque when it shrank. Things do not shrink back the same way, he said.

The General sent me to Siachen so that he could fuck with her, Chef writes. She says nothing has happened. I don't believe a word. She is lying. She has never lied to me before, that bitch.

Chef records a long string of dialogue in bad handwriting at the bottom of the page:

She: 'We slept on separate beds in the bunker. Nothing happened.'

Me: 'What about the tattoo?'

She: 'How many times do I have to tell you — tattoos on the belly get distorted with time.'

Me: 'It was abortion.'

She: 'Not true.'

Me: 'What has the General paid you to keep quiet?'

She: 'You are mad.'

Me: 'If the General is innocent, then I know who did it.'

She: 'Who?'

THE GENERAL'S RATION
No questions asked.

AN OFFICER'S RATION
Wheat flour/rice/bread 450g, sugar 90g,

oil 80g, dal 40g, tea/coffee 9g, salt 20g, porridge 20g, custard powder 7g, corn-flour 7g, ice cream/jelly 7g, condiments 600g/month, vegetables 170g, potatoes 110g, onions 60g, non-citric fruits 230g, citric fruits 110g, eggs 2, chicken 175g, meat dressed 260g, milk 250g, milk (for those who do not eat eggs) 1250g, cheese 50g.

A SOLDIER'S RATION
Wheat flour/rice/bread 620g; sugar 90g, oil 80g, dal 40g, tea/coffee 9g, salt 20g, condiments 600g/month, vegetables 170g, potatoes 110g, onions 60g, fruits 230g, meat dressed 110g, milk (veg) 750g, milk (non-veg) 250g.

I wish I were young again, he writes. Pretty Kashmiri girls, beautiful army wives, nurses — they all fall so easily for the boy. He doesn't even have a full beard. Yet. He is fucking around that *lun*, that prick. Kip.

Perhaps the words were written under the influence of rum. But rum is no excuse.

None of it was true. General Kumar had not *done it*. Chef had no proof. Sahib was a man of highest morals. I, on the other hand, had yet to be with a woman. Other than my erotic reveries I had no experience. My body was simply going to waste. Chef was — that bloody bastard was simply writing lies about Sahib and about me.

Despite his lies I continued to cook for him when he was in hospital. I served him my ration of rum. I fed him his own recipes. I would take the tiffin-carrier to the hospital on bike. He never spoke. He did not speak to anyone. He looked so frail on that metal bed I could not hold anything against him. He lay on the white bed, wrapped in a blanket, his tattooed arm jutting out, stitches on his wrist, and I knew exactly what he was thinking. He was thinking life had ended before it began. The glacier had sucked him dry, that field of snow and ice, that hazaar thousand ton of snow, layers on top of each other, had sat on top of him and demolished his erections. He could no longer get *it* up; *it* had become a bonsai. On his tongue clung the taste of a woman's body and the smell of its hollows, but the glacier had numbed him, and he and his bonsai had even forgotten what it felt like to drown in a woman's fluids. No, up there, twenty thousand feet high, his brain, his organs, were drowning in his own blood. He was thinking there was no justice in the world.

Something fell from his hospital bed. His wallet in which he kept his wife's photo. I picked it up and placed it beside him, and noticed he did not bat his eyes and he kept looking at me with bitterness. His breathing grew heavier, but he did not blink. He was thinking here is a young man, a tall cedar, and he is sleeping around with women twenty-four hours. Kashmiri women were delicate beauties, and the little 'virile Sikh' boy was sleeping around with them, and now and then older army wives, the memsahibs, invited him to their residences and made advances. I felt he wanted me to tell him about my sexual experiences. He wanted to listen to it all but he hated to talk to me. What he did not want to hear from me was the truth, I thought. I was twenty and still a virgin. Me, Kirpal, a virgin.

Outside the sun was brightening the plane trees, and fresh wind was blowing in the valley, and I realized it was time to head out to the bazaar. The streets were red, and on the way I saw women sweeping the leaves into huge piles, filling their big sacks with leaves, and I knew why. They made charcoal in their homes, mixing leaves and sawdust. They used the charcoal in braziers in winter to keep warm. On the way to the bazaar I slowed down my bike and watched the women sweep the leaves. Their breasts alive inside beautiful pherans. I felt empty. I felt like a one big nothing. I was not even worth a soldier's ration.

16

Forgiveness is a strange animal, I say to myself. Not many people on this earth know how to *ask* for forgiveness, and very few know how to truly forgive. I returned to the hospital to ask for forgiveness. I did not really need a bandage, the cut I had on my finger was minor. Some of the wards were absolutely dark. One or two were lit up with emergency lights. There was no power in the hospital, and the whole place smelled of dead cockroaches and chloroform. I waved at her. She ignored me; the sound of her heels clicking throughout the ward was unbearable.

Finally, I stopped her in the corridor.

'Nurse, I have been meaning to say 'sorry' to you.'

'Say it quickly.'

'I was wrong. The way I used to look at you was wrong. It will never happen again.'

She held my arm and I felt she had already forgiven me. I like you a lot, she said, and immediately after saying that she entered the dimly lit ward. The guard saluted her. I lingered until she took a cigarette break and stepped out on the lawn. Only then, when she was gone (and the guard was looking in the other direction), did I step into the ward.

There was a blanket on his face. The only light came from the window in the corner. The blanket heaved up and down. Chef stirred, but did not flap it open. This made my task easier. In a low voice I apologized on two counts. First, for *reading* his journal, and second, for *liking* his woman. Nothing happened between us, Chef. I just told her that I liked her. I did nothing.

I do not recall exactly the words I used, but I apologized and placed the red journal by his pillow and quickly made it to the door. The guard looked at me suspiciously, but didn't utter a word.

Outside in the corridor a man was tapping the floor with his crutches. A thin boy from the Madras regiment in a wheelchair was playing with his saliva, slowly shaking his head left to right and right to left like a machine. The nurse was standing with two or three other nurses. They eyed me curiously.

'I was only trying to have a word with Chef,' I explained.

'Who?' she asked.

'Kishen.'

'But he is not here,' she said.

'Not here?'

'Gone.'

'He left?'

'He put in a request with the colonel for a return to the Rose Glacier.'

'Why did they let him go?'

'Because no one else wanted to go.'

'So who is on the bed?' I raised my voice.

I rarely raise my voice. Perhaps that is why the power returned in the hospital.

There was a commotion in the corridor. *Officers are coming. Officers.* There I saw the colonel and his platoon marching in. The doctor was walking parallel to the colonel in his trussed jacket. The colonel was carrying an inspection stick, and the doctor was smoking a Marlboro.

'Power is very unreliable, sir,' said the doctor to the colonel. The others followed them to the ward. The officers took a long time inside and ordered tea and pakoras.

Half an hour later the hospital orderly stepped out of the ward with an empty tray.

'Major, what tamasha is happening inside?' I asked him.

'We really live in a foreign land, Major. They are dealing with an enemy.'

'An enemy?' I asked.

'Yes, Major. They need an interpreter inside, and no one knows Kashmiri here.'

'I do.'

I knocked on the door.

'Permission to enter, sir?'

'Kip . . . Kirpal?'

'If you do not mind, sir, I know the language. I took lessons, sir.'

'Shahbash,' said the colonel.

He beckoned me inside.

The officers, in proper uniforms and black boots, looked at me in relief as if I had just saved them. The captive lay on the bed. He was a she. The first enemy I ever saw was a she, and already I had apologized to her moments ago on two counts. The first thing I noticed was the unconscious movement of her head. Rapid breathing. Terror in eyes. Peasant feet. The toe ring gleamed in flourescent light. There was a cut on the left foot.

The colonel asked me to occupy the chair next to the enemy's bed. I took a deep breath, then the interrogation began. It was my first time as an interpreter. I asked the questions slowly, she stammered her responses. I do not recall the many unintelligible things she brought to her lips. But the essence has stayed with me.

آ

کہہ مشکل ؟

مشکل چھو نہ کہن جناب ۔

ارم ،ژ چھوئی خبر ژ کیاذی چھو یور آمت ؟

Name?
Nav?
Irem.
Father's name?
Moul sund nav?
Maqbool Butt.
Citizenship?
Shehriyat?
Kashmiri.
Colonel: Ask again.
Citizenship?
Shehriyat?
Kashmiri.
Married?
Khander karith?
Awaa.
Yes.
Husband's name?
Khandaraas nav?

Raza Nomani.
Any issues?
Kahn mushkil?
Khandras manz ché mushkilat aasani . . .
She says, sir, all marriages have problems.
No, what we mean is, does she have children?
Bacchi chhoi kanh?
Na.
No issues, sir.
There was a pause.
Mrs Irem, why are you in India?
Irem, tsé kyazi koruth border cross?
Khooda yi chhum guanha sazaa.
She says, God is punishing her for sins.

The enemy woman started breathing more heavily. The colonel muttered something. She was gasping for breath. The nurse offered her a glass of water. But.

The woman fainted.

The doctor held her wrist for a few seconds, then let it go.

In that entire ward (especially on her bed) my eyes could not locate Chef's red journal. Small insects were climbing up the wall by her bed. I anticipated a trial, a long court martial, at least an inquiry. Empty-handed I returned to the General's kitchen, and my spine shivered with panic when the ADC phoned me:

'General Sahib would like to see you,

173

Kirpal. Report right before golf. Fifteen-thirty hours.'

With great anxiety I walked to the golf-course. I had committed a serious crime. But the General looked in a beautiful mood. He was dressed in civilian clothes. He asked other officers to leave us alone. He was holding an expensive golf stick, and he picked up a white ball.

'You see this, Kirpal.'

'Golf ball, sir?'

'Good.'

'Sir.'

'You see the dimples, Kirpal?'

'See them, sir.'

'Why is the ball dimpled?'

'No idea, sir.'

'Guess?'

'To make it go slower, sir?'

'Faster.'

'Sir is joking.'

'I do not joke, Kip.'

'Sir.'

'Colonel Sahib phoned me. He reported this morning's proceedings at the hospital.'

'Sir.'

'Good job.'

'Thankyousir.'

'Now is your chance to pick up your second rank, and maybe a medal.'

'Sir.'

'Understand me?'

'Not exactly, sir.'

'Find out everything about that enemy woman.'

'How, sir?'

'You are a smart chap.'

'It is an unusual assignment, sir.'

'Delicate assignment, Kirpal.'

'Certainly, sir.'

'Certainly.'

'Sir, if I may, when will I go to the glacier?'

'Things are shaping up. I'll look into this personally. And, Kip — '

'Sir?'

'Everything must remain confidential.'

'Sir.'

'What did we talk about?'

'Balls, sir.'

'Dismiss.'

He narrowed his eyes and hit the ball with his club and I clicked my heels. On the way to my room I thought about all the balls that get lost from the golf course. How many lost golf balls belonged to the army? I wondered. If dimples allowed the balls to go faster, was there a way to make them go slower? Suddenly I started thinking about *fast* and *slow*. Fast and slow in cooking. Fast and slow in the kitchen. This is exactly what we were trying to do in the kitchen.

17

Men in the barracks already knew more about her than I did. She had crossed the river from the enemy side to our camp. One version said she was a suicide bomber, and that her target was schoolchildren. Another version was that she worked for ISI, the enemy spy agency. A third version claimed that she had come to incite the youth of Kashmir to become militants.

I returned the next day. She was wearing a loose pheran, and a third of her body was thickly bandaged. Her head was covered by a scarf. She looked beautiful even in sickness.

'There is a cut on your foot,' I said. 'Why is it not bandaged?'

She stirred her feet as if to say, I know. She withdrew her feet into the blanket as if they were little rats.

'Who did it?'

She did not say anything, so I turned and walked towards the window.

Outside, the troops were marching in the parade ground and the air was dusty.

'In Pakistan you people eat dogs,' I said.

Dust was rising on the road outside. The

troops: *one-two, one-two, one-two.*

'You people eat dogs,' I said loudly.

'No,' she said.

I turned.

Her gaze was fixed on the floor.

'You eat chicken feet . . . snakes . . . lizards . . . you crave . . . '

Chef Kishen had written that the enemy ate cows and buffaloes, and the most repulsive dish on their tables was made by slow cooking a young bull's testicles.

'I know why you are here,' she broke her silence.

Her Kashmiri had a strong Muslim inflection. (The Kashmiri I had learned sounded more like the Kashmiri of pundits.)

'Why?' I asked.

Her eyes were red. She pulled Chef's journal from her blanket. I walked to the head of the bed, and grabbed it from her.

'Did you read?' I was angry at her.

'The person who wrote this,' she said, 'is sometimes very angry and sometimes extremely happy.'

'The journal is written in Hindi.' I raised my voice. 'You lied yesterday. You know Hindi.'

She looked afraid as I uttered those words, raising my voice.

'No, Saheb,' she said.

'You Pakistanis cannot be trusted,' I said.

'I never attended school, Saheb,' she said.

'What does that mean?'

'I cannot read and write, Saheb.'

'Do not call me sahib,' I said. 'Just answer me. If you did not read it, then how can you say that he was sometimes angry and happy?'

'The pen moves fast, then sometimes slow. One can tell,' she said.

Her speech was almost inaudible, and she spoke very slowly. Her words, like a damaged cassette in the tape recorder. This angered me, but I continued to let her speak.

'You do not need to know the language, Saheb, to figure out if the writer of words is angry, sad, or happy.'

'Good,' I said. 'You are illiterate.'

She could not read and write and this made me happy. Her face was intelligent, but she could not read from left to right or right to left and this made me happy. She had no access to Kishen's intimate thoughts. But as I was walking back to the General's kitchen I felt sad that so many people in our land and in the land of our enemy cannot even read and write. I felt pity for her. She was a smart woman but really she was leading the life of a donkey.

She had not touched the tray of food next to her bed. On the wall behind her there were more crawling insects than last time.

'The food, Saheb,' she said, 'is not fit for humans.'

Then. I do not know what made me say: 'I will make sure that you eat well. I will make sure you find out the meaning of real Indian hospitality.'

★ ★ ★

The opportunity to prepare her a proper meal arrived very soon. General Sahib flew to Delhi to meet the COAS, the Chief of Army Staff; and the doctor was away on Internal Security duty. I persuaded the nurse to unlock the doctor's room in the hospital. The room had a beautiful view of distant mountains. They looked completely blue, the Pir Panjals, casting no shadow. Things that are far away always look blue for some unknown reason. Blue is the color of our past. Blue is the color of our wretched past, I say to myself.

It was not my finest accomplishment, but I did my best to feed the 'enemy woman'. I cooked in the General's kitchen, and served her in the doctor's room in the hospital with the nurse present. I do not understand why she still is the 'enemy woman'. To this day, sometimes the phrase slips out of my mouth.

Her name was Irem.

She removed her shoes before stepping on the thick carpet in the doctor's room. Like most Kashmiris she gave the carpet the respect it deserved. The nurse on the other hand kept her dirty shoes on, and I remember the condescending look she gave her patient. There was an open-air cinema not far from the hospital, and most of the staff and guards and non-critical patients were watching a Bombay film there. So the hospital was half empty. The nurse had a shot of rum, and for Irem I made lemonade, and watched from the window.

Music from the open-air cinema wafted into the room. The song playing was about the fickle anger of beautiful women. Irem hesitated to sit on the sofa. So she sat on the carpet, her gaze fixed on the patterns of spiders, lizards, and scorpions embroidered on the beautiful carpet. The colors of the carpet came from vegetable dyes made of roots and berries. The green and indigo and red, although a bit faded, drew me towards them.

The nurse started talking to me in English. I am sleep starved, she said. As if she was the only one who didn't get to sleep. Irem felt increasingly uncomfortable in the room, I could tell. She held her glass as if it was the only thing that could comfort her. Terror was

180

loose in her eyes still. It seemed to me that her lips were moving slightly. There was a cut on her upper lip. She wiped away the condensation with her hand and rolled the lemonade glass the way Buddhists roll prayer wheels in Ladakh.

The nurse stared at her, and the patient started staring at the wall.

There is a photo on the wall.

Irem rises to her feet, and without paying attention to us walks slowly towards the wall and stands before the big black and white photo.

There are five or six women in Islamic garments standing on a sheer cliff. Only their backs are visible. Two or three are praying; one is looking at the immense sky, another is surveying the valley below — the poplars, the willows, the plane trees, the fruit orchards, the lake, and the timber-framed houses. Another stands barefoot, her arms uplifted, palms open in prayer. A ribbon of a cloud is passing by, and it is unclear if the cloud is touching her palm or the folds of the mountain.

It's strange, I am looking at Irem's back and she is looking at the women in the photo. Perhaps there are more than six women. The tall one is hiding the short one, and they are all standing on a cliff. Irem moves slightly to

181

her right; now I see more clearly. At the bottom left corner, a lonely shoe. One small push and it would fall into the valley.

Slowly Irem is becoming a part of that work of art. I do not feel like disturbing. But my breath is becoming heavy.

The nurse begins tapping her feet.

'Irem ji,' I say, switching to Kashmiri, 'I have cooked Rogan Josh for dinner. Halal for you. Non-halal for us.'

No response.

So I start telling her about the recipe I had followed, and then I recall at precisely that moment she turned and muttered something. I ask her to repeat it, and she says: One never uses tomatoes in Rogan Josh.

The nurse asks me to translate.

No tomatoes in Rogan Josh.

This makes her laugh. She laughs at me, the nurse. The enemy doesn't laugh.

'How is that possible?' I say. 'A dish without tomatoes is like a film without sound.'

'No tomatoes,' says Irem.

'Irem ji, please write down *your* recipe of Rogan Josh for me.'

But as soon as I open my mouth, I realize my mistake.

'I am sorry. You cannot write.'

The nurse stares at us.

'But, why is the Rogan Josh so red? If there

are no tomatoes then why is it red?'

Irem remains silent.

'Tell me,' I insist. 'Please.'

'The color comes from the mirchi.'

'But why is the dish so intensely red?'

'Redness comes from the Kashmiri chilies,' she says. 'And mawal flowers.'

'I accept. But, in the absence of tomatoes where does the khatta taste come from?'

'Khatta is due to curds only.'

'I am hungry,' the nurse roars in English, unable to comprehend Kashmiri.

Irem would not sit on the sofa or in the chair. She sat on the carpet. So I spread a white calico sheet on the carpet and transferred the dishes there, and that is how it all began. She closed her eyes and lifted her palms and said a small prayer to Allah and started eating slowly, then picked up speed. Suddenly she remembered she was not alone in the room and slowed down again. She used her left hand to eat, and once or twice licked her fingers.

During dinner she opened up to us and shared her story. She was no longer hesitant.

She had jumped into the river to end her life. To end one's life is against religion, she said. It is a sin. But the life she was leading was worse than death. Her husband and his mother criticized her constantly for not being

183

able to bear a child.

It was a sunny October morning, she told us, and there was taste of bitter almonds in my mouth and suddenly I *knew* what I was going to do. I walked to the high rock by the river, and jumped in. Before I jumped I saw a vision of angels and prayed to Khuda to please kill me. Now, I am being punished by him for wanting to commit *khud-qushi*.

I did not drown. Instead I floated down the river to the Indian side, where I was fished out by a border guard. I told the guard that I was from *border-cross* and that I was not a rebel. Where is your passport and visa? he asked me. Why have you entered the country illegally? he asked me. It was then he handed me over to the military, and the military sent me to this hospital, she said.

Irem's pheran had a strange embroidery on it. She had jumped into the river wearing that very pheran, and it had clung to her body during her *journey* from the enemy's land to our land. That night, after listening to her story, I biked to the General's residence not only with the tiffin-carriers and cutlery, but also with Irem's pheran. She had stained the pheran during dinner, and the nurse had asked me to drop the garment at the washerman's hut on the way.

Cycling to the General's residence I kept

184

returning to everything that had transpired during the dinner. It was like replaying a black and white film again and again. Every attempt was unsatisfactory. So I would start again. Fail again. Start again. I took the pheran to my room. When my assistant was not around I smelled the garment. It smelled of the sweat of a beautiful woman. The embroidered pattern on the hem was almost like a leaf. I did not know the name of the pattern, but a few months later a different woman would reveal to me the name of it. It is called *paisley*, she would tell me. Back in those days (and nights) the more attention I paid to paisley, the more I felt that the pattern ought to be a symbol of something.

That was the first night Kashmir felt like home to me. Despite that I lay in bed with my shoes and uniform. The assistant reminded me once or twice to change my clothing, but I asked him to bugger off, and I kept recalling the five minutes I spent absolutely alone with Irem. The nurse had stepped out to attend a patient in the ward, and I had spent five full minutes alone with Irem.

'I am sorry,' I said. 'This morning I raised my voice.'

'No problem,' she said.

'Is there something you would like me to do?'

185

'No.'

'I would like to help you.'

'No.'

'Please tell me.'

'If possible, bring me the Qur'an.'

'But?'

'But what?'

'You cannot read.'

'I can hold the Qur'an.'

There was an awkward silence. Her eyes were red. She needed the book more than she needed my food.

'There are many varieties of Muslims?' I asked. 'I have heard about the Shia, the Sunni and the Sufi. What kind of a Muslim are you?'

'Homeless,' she said.

Her response eased some of the tension between us.

'You see that mountain up there, where the bright lights are?' I pointed through the window. 'That is where my room is.'

She nodded.

'I have lived there, in the barracks, for a while now. Sometimes when I am down in the valley, or here in the hospital at night, the mountain up there looks like a huge aircraft. When the lights are turned on in the evening it appears as if the aircraft is ready to depart.'

She remained silent. I kept talking. Now that I think about it what a fool I made of myself. To this day I have not figured out how to stop talking when in the presence of a beautiful woman.

'On certain nights,' I said, 'I hear the sound of sirens, ambulances rushing towards this hospital, and I feel as if the aircraft is about to explode.'

She moved closer to the window, carrying her plate of Rogan Josh. There was a slight limp in her walk.

'You talk like men in Bombay films.'

The way she said this so fearlessly, so unexpectedly, impressed me a lot.

'The mountain is visible from our side also,' she continues. 'From the other side of the river, we too get to see it. The children in our village point at the memorial at the very top of the mountain. Have you been there?'

'No,' I say.

She turns. She is so beautiful. I can't point at a concrete detail of her face and say *that is why she is beautiful*. I just turn away my eyes.

'Mihirukula's memorial,' she says.

I force my gaze and desperately try to find a flaw in that beauty. I fail. Then, I succeed. There are big gaps between her teeth. Her teeth are not beautiful.

'Mihirukula?'

'The White Hun's memorial,' she says.

'The Hun?'

She speaks very slowly, revealing her teeth. She tells me something women don't usually tell men they have just met. There was a garden in our village. Now it is a ruin. The White Hun came with a huge army of elephants. Elephants? I clarify. Yes, she says. Elephants. One of them fell from the cliff, 10,000 feet below. The Hun loved it. He was amused by the shriek of the falling animal. With one little finger he commanded his men to kick off four hundred elephants purely for his amusement. Trumpet-like sounds. For days afterwards my ancestors heard the echoes of dying creatures.

Then all was silence.

In my village the ambulance sirens remind us of elephants, she says.

Why did you tell me this?

She tries to sit down. The plate falls from her trembling hand, staining her iridescent pheran. Then the spoon lands in slow motion on the carpet. Why did you tell me? You Kashmiris from top-man to bottom-man are all anti-India. Her eyes turn red like a brick. Saheb, I am not like that, she stammers. Some militants in our village are planning to kill. But I don't want Kashmir back if most of us end up dead.

'Who are the men going to kill?'

'The biggest officer of your military.'

188

'The General?'

'I think so.'

'How do you know?'

'I heard it in the village. Please save him. His car must never pass the Zero Bridge.'

'Not a word more.'

The nurse was angry with Irem when she returned. There was Rogan Josh on the carpet, and its long trail was visible on Irem's pheran. She asked me to step out for a minute, and when I re-entered the room Irem had changed into a striped kurta-pyjama. She looked uncomfortable in the oversize pyjama-kurta. The drawstring dangled. I turned my gaze downwards and focused only on the carpet, her feet, and her words.

Next morning I woke up with the enemy's pheran under my pillow. It had a mysterious odor. I sent my assistant to the bazaar and washed the pheran along with my clothes, and dried it on the line in my room, hidden between my clothes. While ironing I was very careful not to break the buttons at the back. Two were missing. While ironing I thought, isn't it funny that in the Hindi language the word for *iron* and the word for *woman* is one and the same. I sprinkled water on the garment and ironed till all the wrinkles disappeared.

In the evening I looked at the mountain

again. The plane trees were turning color. The mountain carried no memory of the falling elephants. If there was something falling it was a red leaf, falling very slowly, without a shriek. I cycled down the mountain with the neatly folded pheran in my kit. When I see her, I thought, I must tell her to stand by the window again, and look at the slopes in the light of the evening. What makes some leaves linger on trees in autumn? I wanted to ask many questions. I wanted to know what was she like before she got married? What was she like as a girl?

How did other strangers respond to her? What were the foods she disliked? Did she have enough to eat? Who taught her to cook? I wanted to ask her all these questions and know all the answers.

When I got to the hospital I parked my bike and walked into the ward. But she was gone. I did not know what to do. So. I cycled to the Hazratbal Mosque via the Zero Bridge. There were people on the bridge. Two cops were guarding the structure, the green trusses. The river was muddy and overflowing. The mosque was in the low-lying area just six hundred yards from the bridge. Flooding was a possibility. An old woman was feeding pigeons inside the compound of the mosque and I removed my shoes and walked barefoot on marble towards her. She was old, but still beautiful. Women in Kashmir were always beautiful. I had no idea how to buy a Qur'an and as I proceeded towards her I noticed the men looking at me suspiciously as if perhaps in my turban I had come to steal the relic. Their eyes were fierce. Their bodies were wet and dripping; it seemed as if they had just stepped out of the hamaam. The old woman pointed her finger towards the store in the street. You do not buy Qur'ans inside the mosque, she said. Then she resumed feeding the pigeons. Patiently she tore the bread into tiny morsels. There were thousands of them, pigeons, shitting in the same compound where they were being fed.

Allah u Akbar
Allah u Akbar
Allah u Akbar
Allah u Akbar
Ash-hadu Alla Ilaha-ill-allah
Ash-hadu Alla Ilaha-ill-allah
Ash-hadu Anna Mohammadan Rasul-allah
Ash-hadu Anna Mohammadan Rasul-allah
Hayya-Alas-Salat
Hayya-Alas-Salat
Hayya-Alal-Falah
Hayya-Alal-Falah
Allah u Akbar

Allah u Akbar
La-ilaha ill-allah

The boy at the store was not paying attention to *azan*. He was solving math problems. His Philips radio was playing qawalis, Shahbaz Qalandar, and to this day I am able to recall the problem he was struggling with. Years before I, too, had to deal with the same complicated equation in school.

$$X^3 + Y^3 = L^3 + M^3 = 1729$$

I coughed. He looked up. His nose was running.

'Do you sell the Qur'an?'

'How many?' he asked as if I was going to buy them by the dozen.

'Kid,' I said, 'first explain to me the proper way to give respect to the Qur'an.'

'Are you buying?'

'Of course,' I said. 'One.'

'Then I will teach you,' he said.

The boy wrapped the book in a velvet cloth.

'Wash your hands before praying,' he said.

'Same thing,' I said. 'We do the same in Sikhism.'

He didn't seem interested in learning about my religion and returned to math. I almost told him the correct answer, but changed my mind. 1729. The smallest number that can be expressed as the sum of two cubes in two different ways.

X = 1
Y = 12
L = 9
M = 10

* * *

The man who first solved this problem was the South Indian mathematician Ramanujan. He was a genius and he solved this problem on his deathbed at the age of twenty-nine. In school the teacher used to tell us many stories about math. She also told us that zero — the most important ingredient of math — was invented in our own country, only later the concept migrated to Arab countries.

It was getting dark. I cycled back to the camp with the Qur'an in the front carrier. In my kit there were apples and a trout wrapped in a paper. Nearing the camp I noticed something I had seen several times before but had never thought to be important. Not far from the bridge the road rises sharply, and from an elevated spot, while pedaling breathlessly, I saw sudden points of light, I witnessed the precise moment the electric lights were being turned on in our country and in the enemy's country. The enemy turned on their lights (on the brown mountains it had occupied) at precisely the same time, I realized, we turned on the lights on our mountains. Both sides declared night at the same time, I thought, despite the time difference. I stopped my bike and waited by the railing for a long time, and thought about the kitchens on both sides of the border, the culinary similarities and differences, and I thought about rain, which was now falling, too, on both sides, making the lines fuzzier and fuzzier.

General Sahib's residence hummed with its yellow lights. It was the second brightest place on our side of the border, I noticed. The brightest was the Governor's mansion on the hill, shimmering with mystery.

That night as I served tea in Sahib's room, I felt I was at two places at once. I was on the Zero Bridge looking at the bright lights of Sahib's residence and I was inside as well, inside the residence holding a tray. The General was back from his travels. Perhaps he, too, felt he was in two places at once. I knocked at the door.

'Come in.'

Sahib separated himself from the book he was reading.

'Kip!'

'Sir.'

He requested me to switch on the fluorescent light.

'I must tell you,' he said, 'the turmeric you add in the tea is helping my stomach ache.'

'Thank you, sir.'

'And Kip — '

'Sir.'

'More on the enemy woman?'

'She is clean, sir.'

Sahib took slow sips of tea as I told him Irem's drowning story.

'Something else?'

I wanted to, but I could not reveal the bombing story because I was afraid for Irem.

'No, sir.'

'Why are you trembling?'

'Sorry, sir. Been cycling in the rain, sir.'

'Any knowledge of terrorist activity?'

'No, sir,' I lied. 'But, we must investigate more.'

'Why?'

'Sahib, perhaps if we slow down the investigation.'

'Slow?'

'So far I have investigated very fast, sir. But I plan to proceed slowly from now on. The way it is with the golf balls, sir.'

'Kip. Sunno. Your assignment is over.'

'Over, sir?'

'No need to interrogate the enemy any further.'

'But, sir, I have just started.'

'Kip, we have excavated enough information. Now the interrogation must stop.'

I kept my eyes fixed on the spine of the book now shut on the table top.

'Sir.'

'The colonel will soon issue a commendation certificate to you.'

'But, sir — '

'You may go now.'

'Sir.'

Every morning I would check with Sahib's car driver about the routes he was planning to follow. The Zero Bridge, because of the rain, was never on the route and this was reassuring. But I was really worried, and for that reason I cycled in civilian clothes to the city post office and mailed an unsigned note to the army HQ warning about a possible attack on General Kumar. The letter had immediate effect. The army beefed up security around the bridge, interrogated the locals and raided many Kashmiri houses in the area. A journalist wrote confidently in the national paper, Peace has returned to the valley. Days later when the General's black military car (with a flag and four stars) passed the Zero Bridge nothing happened. Three seconds later the bridge exploded.

The river carried away the ripped parts, the blown-up arches, and for days the waters looked high and muddy and black, and not just because of the rain.

The driver of the car told me later: Major, the moment the bridge exploded I felt as if my heart had leaped out of my chest. But I also felt the invisible hand of God protecting us. I cannot forget the roar, the rain of wood and metal and fire. The car started flying. Then booom, it fell. I kept driving. The General shouted (from the back seat): *Tej. Tej. Fast. Faster.* My foot was on the gas, hammering it. Look at this hole in the body of the car, Major. God gave us only a little hole in the rear, and a few damaged parts inside. God made me drive fast. Are you with me, Major?

Yes, yes, I said.

God is great, Major.

She is clean, I said to myself. Irem is clean.

18

In the kitchen the trout stared at me for many days. Fish can be cut any which way. So it is better than meat, I thought. No quarrel about halal or non-halal. Trout I had thought was the best way to have *conversation* with the enemy. But Sahib asked me to stop all *conversation*.

Outside, it kept raining against the window, corroding the cutlery inside. The rain mocked me, for many days rain lashed. The eyes of that fish mocked me. But. The inclement weather had a reverse effect on my cooking. The mushiness in the air prevented the drying. I sprinkled fresh coriander and roasted caraway seeds on the tender, moist fish. The orderly, who was my friend, delivered the tiffin-carrier in the hospital. He delivered the holy book as well. She did not send any message for me. But she had kissed the Qur'an, the orderly told me.

'She refused to eat the fish, Major.'

'Did she say something?'

'The nurse was standing close to the bed and the enemy woman said (using signs and gestures) that she had no intention to eat for the next forty days.'

'Why don't you say it is Ramadan?' I raised my voice.

'Did I do something wrong, Major?' he apologized.

'No,' I said.

'Major,' he said.

'Please leave me alone.'

'She said one thing else, Major.'

'What?'

'When she is eating normally she feels hungry around noon. But now that she is eating abnormally, I mean now that she is fasting, at noon she feels thirsty only.'

'What else?'

'That's all, Major,' he said. 'Now I will go away.'

'Yes,' I said. 'Don't show me your face again.'

★ ★ ★

I see myself unable to sleep, waking up with a dry throat. In my dream I am hungry, I have not eaten for days and I am in a classroom in Pakistan and the teacher (who is eating a kebab) is angry with me. On the blackboard words are written in Urdu in thick chalk, I notice as the teacher walks towards my bench, holding a stick in his right hand. The

199

sound of his boots approaching me is growing louder. Now we are standing face to face, his kebab breath gets trapped in my nostrils. The teacher is wearing a military uniform, medals on his breast. General President Musharraf? I ask. Open your palm, he says. What's my crime? You are sitting next to a female student, he says. I turn my neck: the girl. I survey quickly her face. She is absolutely silent, her lips sealed tight. She is not eating. I feel sick to my stomach. Open your palm, he says. The General hits my palm with the stick. The girl shuts her eyes, her body shakes. The stick keeps hitting me over and over. Suddenly the girl starts laughing. Don't laugh, I say. Don't laugh at me, I request. Not here.

All through rain (and Ramadan) there were dinners. The kitchen grew very busy because of a stream of visitors who came to congratulate Sahib for having survived the explosion. The chief of security was suspended and four other officers responsible for the protection of the bridge were imprisoned. Many more local houses were raided to hunt the terrorists.

Gen Sahib had little time for himself. He was also preoccupied with a high-level court martial. The court martial would bring its own stream of officers to the residence. I found myself a bit stressed, sleeping barely four or five hours. The ADC instructed me to cook Punjabi karhi-chawal, mitha shalgum, and saag maki-di-roti for Brigadier Pash, the presiding officer of the court martial. Pash's nickname was *BapuGandhi*; the Brigadier was renowned for his honesty and vegetarianism.

'Here comes the famous Brigadier Pash.' Sahib shook his hand in the drawing room.

From behind the curtain I overheard the conversation between the two men.

'Is there an evidence?'

'Not on paper — '

The glasses tinkled and plates clattered and spoons rattled, but I can't forget the syllables of Gen Sahib's crisp voice.

'The man is innocent,' he told the presiding officer. 'Make sure his career is not stained.'

'But, sir,' said the Brigadier. 'I am assuming the army wants to know. Even if we are not interested — the whole thing has been recorded on a spy camera. Three press reporters posing as arms dealers from the UK and the USA visited Colonel Chowdhry's residence and offered him bottles of whiskey. If you are going to bribe me *chutiya*, the colonel told them, at least bribe me with 5 crore rupees and Blue Label. Black Label won't do. Then there is the coffin scam — '

'This is a set-up, Brigadier Pash,' said General Sahib. 'Don't you see? Images these days can be manipulated by technology. There is no written evidence, no real evidence against him. The colonel would never sell our boys for the price of Blue Label.'

The civilian papers were filled with news of Col Chowdhry of 5 Mountain Division. He had been involved in several scams, the latest one being the coffin scam. The colonel had bought hundreds of aluminum coffins from an American company at 200 dollars apiece. He had charged the army 1800 dollars apiece. More dead Indian soldiers at the front meant more profits for the colonel and his politico friends in Delhi and Washington. One or two papers held General Sahib responsible for the coffin scam. But Sahib was innocent really. The colonel had taken advantage of Sahib's trust. Despite that, Sir was trying to save the man.

'Do keep him under a watch. But don't start anything new. He is clean. Let him go.'

'But, sir, are you asking me to lie?'

'We must protect the morale of our army.'

'If I lie, sir, I'll feel bad. And if I tell the truth, I'll feel bad. What should I do, sir?'

'Nothing.'

'Nothing, sir?'

'Eat the food, Brigadier. Do you like the *saag*?'

'Excellent, sir.'

It rained for thirty-nine days. Then it stopped and one night it started raining again. From the kitchen window I heard the sounds and inhaled the smell of falling leaves. During day the trees looked wet and bare and dead, but at night the pointed branches moved as if alive. Rain fell on the yellow lights of Alpha Mess and the Quarter Guard where the court martial was to take place. The trials didn't mean much to me then, I am embarrassed to admit, not as much as sleep, and sleep was a rare commodity in the army.

Something happened in the hospital.

Irem found a strand of hair in the dinner I sent her a week before the Eid. The guards told me: The enemy woman wept uncontrollably, Major. The nurse had to give her a needle. The enemy took that strand of hair out of the bowl of dal, Major. She raised her hand high and held it in the light and looked at it like a detective and then she started weeping, Major.

I didn't know what to do with Irem. While cooking, I listened to Chef Kishen's German music. It went fast, then slow. Fast, and slow again. The notes swelled and shrank, and made me move deeper and deeper inside something beautiful. Then I was rising like a fish in a dead lake, the ripples spreading. During break I walked down to the hospital with the tape recorder in my kit. Troops were marching in the rain. They were marching on the muddy road, too, lined with military vehicles. Drops were dancing on the license plates. I did not care about my fears. It seemed natural to go to her. I stepped into the ward. She had fewer bandages and looked stronger sitting up in the metal bed, her head covered by the same scarf, and for the first time I realized that her features resembled the Bombay actress Waheeda. The same chiseled face, the same nose, the same cheeks. In Irem's left hand there was a golf ball. She was concentrating on the ball. Outside the window rain was falling on bare trees. I figured the ball must have entered the room through the window. She was examining the ball's dimples. Without moving her eyes she greeted me.

'Salaam.'

'Salaam,' I said.

She kept studying the ball.

'With balls like these,' I explained, 'the sahibs play golf on the lawns.'

Her fingers tried to squeeze the ball gently the way people squeeze fruits before buying.

'The dimples are there for a reason,' I said.

'I know,' she said.

'You know?'

'They make the ball go faster.'

'Who are you?' I asked.

She smiled but stopped short of responding to me. Outside the trees looked dark and wet and naked.

'Listen,' I said. 'You are a smart woman. But there are things you do not know. And that is why you waste your tears. I have come to reveal something about myself to you. If you do not know it already, then you must get to know it,' I said. 'In one single breath I would like to tell you. Here. Look at my face.'

She fixed her gaze on my boots, not my face.

'Look at my face,' I said.

It seemed natural to do what I did next. I removed my turban. I revealed the knot of hair on my head. She raised her eyes and surveyed me curiously.

'I have long hair.'

I don't recall if she dropped the ball or it fell on its own from her hand. The ball bounced several times on the floor before rolling and then coming to a stop, becoming absolutely still.

My hair tumbled to my knees.

'That is why you found the strand in the dal,' I explained. 'You wept for one big nothing.'

'So they inform you of everything about me.'

'Because I would like to know you,' I said.

'Liar.'

'No.'

'What do you want to know about me?'

'Everything.'

She eyed my long hair with enormous curiosity. It was the first time she looked right through me.

'There are women who envy me,' I said, 'because I have hair longer than theirs.'

She continued gazing at me with the same curiosity. She looked right through me, and slowly her hands unknotted the scarf on her head. Slowly she let it go.

'Hair,' she said.

My gaze followed the movement of the scarf as it fell on the floor.

Then I heard her forced, convulsive laughter. I raised my eyes and observed: they had shaved off her hair. She broke out laughing before she wept. Like a child. Why did they shave off her hair? I asked myself. Why did *we* shave her head?

My eyes, too, welled up. Me, wearing very long hair, and this woman mourning the loss of her hair. Her scarf on the floor, and my turban on the table. I felt as if the two *things*, the scarf and the turban, were talking to each other.

Before I walked back to the kitchen I

retrieved the tape recorder from my kit and left it by her bed.

'I am leaving this music machine for you,' I said. 'The top is broken, so be careful. Look at my fingers. Here. This is the button you push to play. Push the last button to eject. Like this.'

Her gaze remained fixed on the broken top. I pressed the button.

She listened to the music. A bit startled at first, the expression on her face changed many times until she smiled. I noticed again the small insects climbing up the whitewashed wall by her bed. The insects were vibrating too. I wanted to ask her many questions, and I had imagined she would request in that Muslim Kashmiri inflection of hers 'Play it again! Play it again!', but listening to those sounds she fell asleep.

mein bowznaav bayyi akki latté
akki latté bayyi
bowznaav
mein
winekya . . .

Sleeping, her hand lay extended. It appeared as if her hand was drawn, there was the sense of a painting. Her hand was woven into the foreign music. When the tape stopped her breathing became audible. There was a certain contradiction between the happiness on her sleeping face and the happiness of her dreams and her unhappy waking hours. What was she dreaming of? Was it wind or water or snow?

I returned to the kitchen with her untouched plate. She didn't eat that day. If by shaving her hair off we meant to humiliate her, we had succeeded.

19

In November General Sahib flew on a helicopter with the Defense Minister to inspect the two battalions on Siachen Glacier. He took me along. Kip, he said, Minister Sahib and I will inspect the troops and you inspect the kitchens on the glacier.

Yessir.

In the helicopter it was cramped. The pilot made me sit on the seat right behind Sahib. The Minister and the General talked about matters connected to the security of our country, using code words like Peak 18 or NJ9842. From one white mountain to the next we flew like an eagle and I felt an intense pressure in my balls. My vertigo was growing more and more intense. Sahib, I almost cried out to him. Sahib, I can't take it. He didn't hear. I focused my gaze on his polished shoes and socks, and perhaps it was his black socks which comforted me. I shut my eyes and started thinking about the kitchen trainee. Two days ago the man had come to the kitchen and on his first afternoon he had used Sahib's charcoal black sock to strain tea. I had scolded him on the spot. Major, I did nothing wrong, he had defended himself. Major, this is how we strain tea in our village. Bewakuf!

★ ★ ★

'Why are you laughing, Kirpal?' demanded the General in the helicopter. In my nose was trapped the smell of dirty laundry tea.

'Sahib, it is just that I cannot be myself in the presence of such high mountains, such everlasting snow.'

The helicopter moved up in spirals and my lungs felt the lack of air. Suddenly we fell a few hundred feet. The machine dropped altitude without warning.

'Minister, sir, the chap lost his father during the recon operation of NJ9842,' said the General.

'My sympathies with you, my boy,' said the Minister.

The helicopter landed on the glacier helipad. Siachen is the second coldest place on earth. Two senior officers whisked the General and the Minister to a special tent.

Kishen appeared out of the thick fog and cold to receive me. He had one star less and I had one star more on my epaulettes, but the whole operation was a farce. He was my senior and I his junior, but our ranks held a different meaning. Our ranks said that I was his senior and he my junior. Kishen clicked his heels and saluted me and said 'Welcome' and to that welcome added the word 'sir'. I extended my hand nervously. He hesitated to shake it at first, but changed his mind and crushed my hand like cloves of garlic.

He took me inside the white arctic tent. We sat down. Wind was howling outside, flapping the canvas. The kerosene bukhari was burning. His face was visible in the flames of the bukhari. There were dark rings beneath his eyes. He suddenly appeared older than his age.

'So you have come,' he said.

'Sir.'

'Don't call me, sir, you little . . . '

'Can we begin the inspection?'

'You little Sikh, you think you have come here to inspect the rat's alley? Do we have a cockroach problem in the kitchen? Do we know how to make Japani food? What are you going to do? How are you going to start?'

'General Sahib asked me to . . . '

'You toady of the General.'

'Can we begin?'

'What begin?'

'The General would like to know the problems in the kitchen.'

'What problems? We got no problems.'

211

His mind was elsewhere. Just then a brown dog entered the tent. It shook the snow off and came to sniff me. For no reason it jumped and licked my parka. I patted its head and suggested a walk, and to my surprise Chef stood up. We muffled ourselves and stepped out, and I still recall the sound our rubber boots made on brittle ice, and the dog's panting. Wind struck our cheeks and he kept moving his arms up and down in the air, under the sky, and we were so high up we had essentially become the sky, and he moved his gloved hands up and down in air, and said this is how in Chef Muller's country they conducted music. I am conducting music, he said.

This music makes me think of the epic Mahabharata, he said. When they grew old the Pandavas headed towards the mountains, climbing higher and higher towards the Gates of Heaven. No one followed them, only a stray dog. The brothers fell one by one on the steep trail. Only Yudhister, the eldest, and the dog made it to the Gates. You can enter, said the gatekeeper. But the animal is not allowed in Heaven. The dog followed me all the way, protested Yudhister, my brothers gave up, but this creature was my constant companion. I will not enter alone.

'Did he?' I asked.

Chef was silent. He walked me through loose snow to a deep crevasse, and pointed at the seracs (on the other side), and said that the crevasse was really the mouth of the glacier, and the seracs were its white teeth. This is how the glacier eats, he said.

The dog started running around the crevasse.

'Don't worry,' he said.

'How deep is it, Chef?'

He took a pebble out of his parka and dropped it.

We heard a sound twenty seconds after the pebble was lost in the crevasse.

'What do you think about the glacier?'

'From the helicopter it looked like a giant man's tongue outside his mouth, licking a woman's navel. Siachen was a big tattoo on a pregnant belly.'

He stared at me.

'You read my journal,' he said.

I didn't respond.

'You little Sikh, you *ma-dar-chod*, you read my journal?'

It was so cold words froze in my mouth. Suddenly I saw the glacier as a huge living organism about to claim me, about to claim us all. This organism paralyzed my thoughts. Father, I cried. Father, I screamed.

'Hit me,' I said. 'Please hit me.'

He put his arm around my shoulder. I felt it barely because of all the layers between us.

'Hit me.'

'I have already hit you,' Chef laughed.

It was a wild laugh. White fumes came out of his mouth. His lips were cracked.

'Hit me,' I said.

'I already hit you. Not enough? It hurts real hard where I hit you. Don't you know? Don't you? I hit you with my writing.'

'I am confused,' I said.

'You *read* my notebook because *you* wanted to read it. But I would have given it to you anyways. I, too, wanted you to *read* it.'

'You are joking, Chef?'

'Does it hurt?'

'But, why? Why did you want me to read it?'

'Because . . . '

Before he could respond I felt my anger rising.

'Because otherwise men are strangers to one other,' he said. 'Even if we carry the same wounds, we remain strangers. We can't express ourselves properly. Not even our anger. I was able to write certain things down because I was writing them for you. I was angry at you. Angry at myself. Angry at so many people. But.'

'But, what?'

'I am no longer. I request only one thing.

Please don't be angry at me. You are not just *one man*. I have always seen you as *two*. You are my beloved, and you are also my witness.'

'Witness?'

'Now I can leave.'

'Where?'

'When I am gone, you must not mourn me.'

It was then he shared with me the *plan*. Standing by the crevasse he shared the details in strict confidence. I begged him not to carry it out. I am not going to be a party to this, I said. Listen to me, he said. If your father were alive, he would have done exactly what I am going to do. Exact same action. Listen to me, you Sikh. I was your teacher. When a teacher opens his mouth the student listens. When a teacher asks for dakshina the student must provide the fees. Do you know the Mahabharata? he asked. It is very long, I said. What do you mean *long*? You kids don't read it these days, but let me tell you in the Mahabharata most people believe that the main story is brothers fighting brothers over the kingdom. Nothing can be further from the truth. The real story is that of the black boy. The low-caste boy. The boy was born a talented archer and he approached the Brahmin teacher to advance his skill. The Brahmin used to teach archery to the king's sons. He said no to the black boy. So, the boy returned to the jungle, he made a clay figure of the Brahmin, and in the presence of the clay figure and a solitary tree the boy taught himself archery, he became more skilled than the king's sons, as a result they grew jealous and their teacher grew worried, so the Brahmin approached the black boy and demanded his fee. The boy was pleased, the *teacher* had accepted him finally as his student, he was willing to give anything the guru asked for. One is supposed to offer one's life if the teacher asks for it. The Brahmin did not ask the boy his life, all he wanted was the boy's right thumb. That very instant the *student* took a sharp knife and cut off his right thumb (which was as black as his face) and offered it to his teacher. He became a cripple, he was never able to practice archery again. Understand? I am not asking you, Kirpal, to offer me your thumb or the fingers of your hand, all I need you to do is this one thing. Be my witness.

I could not return Chef Kishen's gaze, which penetrated through me. Life is so precious, I said. I know, he said. Will any harm come to General Sahib? I asked him again. No, he assured me, no harm, not a single hair that belongs to him will be harmed.

By the end of the day Chef was *gone*.

Khatam.

Finished.

20

Everything is ready. The inspection of two battalions on the glacier is done. The snow-scooter ride is over. There was a fog on Siachen the previous night, I heard. Now the fog has gone, the peaks are visible, K2 is visible, the sun is bright, so bright it brings black dots in front of eyes. The sky is cobalt blue.

The General and the Defense Minister have started eating lunch. The two men are in the Officers' tent. The colonel sends a boy to the kitchen. The Defense Minister would like to have a word with the cook. I look at Chef Kishen. He has done the cooking with his own hands. I look at his four assistants, then at Chef again. He surveys me with piercing eyes. I notice the determination in them, and that is why I decide to go ahead with the *plan*.

I go bundled to the Officers' tent. There is sushi in front of them. I overhear the General explaining to the Minister the art of growing bonsai trees. I overhear the Minister's question on 'tent windows'. Gen Sahib's response: 'The Swiss have developed new technology, sir. As I mentioned before, from here we are able to see the men outside, but they can't see us . . . Yes, yes, Kip, come in.' I salute. 'Shahbash, Kip! Good food!' I tell Sahib that Chef Kishen did all the cooking. If anyone deserves praise — it is him. Not me. Briefly I survey the sushi on the table, and my mouth waters. Cuttlefish. Hamaguri. Sashimi-Salmon Rose. The General asks me to bring along Kishen.

I return to fetch him.

They are ready.

Chef Kishen's four assistants salute him. They call him *Commander*. The Commander is in full military dress. His shoes are impeccably polished.

It is minus 49 outside. Useless tears in my eyes.

On the way Commander Kishen stops by the Soldiers' tent, and stands before the red letter-box. From his pocket he pulls out two letters, one addressed to his children, and the other to his wife. He laughs a bit. Like a good man who is forced by circumstances to commit evil in a Bombay film.

They march to the Officers' tent. I go with them.

Savdhan.

Vishram.

They march over the crunching snow, faces

hidden, aprons whipping.

Left. Right. Left. Right.

Dayan. Bayan. Dayan. Bayan.

White plumes come out of our mouths.

We stop outside the Swiss tent.

I enter. The Commander and his assistants wait outside. Then: 'Sir, Chef Kishen here,' he says. 'Permission to enter?'

'Permission granted,' says the General.

'Sir, my junior staff members are with me. Permission to enter?'

'Permission granted,' says the General.

'Kya naam hai terah?' asks the Defense Minister.

'Chef Kishen, sir.'

'Oh the embassy-wallahs gave him this name. Kishen was trained there. The chap knows cooking very well, sir.' The General turned to the Defense Minister.

'Good food,' says the Minister. 'Shabash.'

'Thank you, sir.'

'Were you trained at the Japanese Embassy?'

'Years ago, sir.'

'I must say this is one of the finest sushis I have ever had. The fish melted in my mouth right away.'

'Thank you, sir.'

'Kishen, what food do you think is best for this glacicr area?'

'Sashimi, for officers, sir.'

'Certainly.'

'To make sashimi, sir, the cut is important. It is the cut, sir, that is most important. Knives are very important.'

'You chaps know it all.'

'Permission to display the knives, sir?'

'Permission granted.'

The table is bright. Strong light filters through the tent window. The Commander's assistants place the knives one by one on the square of light. The two sahibs examine the shiny knives.

When the knives are returned, the Commander gives a quick nod to his assistants. They rush towards the General and the Minister and tie them with ropes to the post and seal their lips with a tape. They do exactly the same thing to me. Everything is going according to the *plan*. I am to behave as if I am not with them.

The colonel (standing guard) outside senses something fishy inside the tent. He tries to enter, but is rebuffed. He tries again. 'You asshole. If something happens to the General . . . ' One of the Commander's four assistants says loudly that no harm would come to the General and the Minister and Chef Kirpal. We have three demands, he tells the colonel. Demand one: Gather the two battalions of troops outside the General's tent. Demand two: Commander Kishen will address the troops, and the troops must listen to him in complete silence. Demand three: the media and press must be allowed to witness the address.

The colonel is a rational man. He agrees to the demands.

He sounds the emergency bugles. He assembles the entire two battalions below the General's tent in twelve minutes. From inside the tent we can hear the sound of boots hitting snow and ice. I see a five-three-five troop formation.

Half an hour passes by. Still no sign of media.

'Colonel, you asshole . . . don't play games with us.'

'Media is on its way,' he says fast. 'I have radioed them thrice.'

The Commander steps out. One assistant follows behind him. Inside we hear the metallic click of a rifle's safety being released. But there is no fire. Three assistants keep an eye on three hostages inside the tent.

Soon a helicopter is hovering in the air. It lands. The flaps of the tent flutter. We hear the rotors come to a stop. TV and paper reporters and photographers have arrived. Sitting so close to mc the General and the Minister look like two little rats. I try to free myself. My ropes are not as tight as theirs. Freeing myself is not part of the plan. I feel for once like changing the foolish plan.

Outside, Commander Kishen begins his address. The wind is howling like mad. He begins softly but soon raises his voice. The wind. He begins by thanking all the men who had died defending our country.

Thank you, soldiers of 8th Battalion, 7 Mountain Regiment; and 23rd Battalion, 15 Corps, says the Commander. The army is the soul of our country, he says. But that old tradition of camaraderie and humanity has died out in our regiments.

We have officers who have opened big hotels and malls in Delhi and Gurgaon. We have officers who make money out of selling rations, make money out of recruitment. We have men who are involved in coffin scams. More dead Indians at the front means more profits for officers and their friends in Delhi. The question I ask today is: Are we dying for nothing? Did so many of our fellows die for nothing? One big nothing? We feed the army, we work hard, and those at the very top have failed us. I would like you to protest this. I would like you to think hard. Ask what are we doing on this glacier, on these Icefields? Ask why do we want to melt away this glacier? The kerosene and other poisons we discard on the glacier end up flowing in our holy rivers. For a long time we Indians have believed that the gods live up in the mountains. Why are we now wrecking the home of our gods? Why do we need Kashmir? Ask. Does Kashmir need us? We shit on the glacier, and the shit freezes and we have to break it with the rifles. And I say the same thing to the bastards on the other side. What are they dying for, the Pakistanis? This ice is no place for human beings. It has wasted the lives of our finest soldiers. We shit on . . .

He is trying very hard to explain himself, something that he has been processing for a while. But the soldiers of the two assembled battalions are not very responsive. Soon more cheetah helicopters start hovering over the glacier. The soldiers boo and whistle and create a racket, and the Cheetah helicopters create a racket, blowing snow in their eyes and creating deafening noise. Minus 55.

The soldiers are unable to hear him properly. Two more helicopters appear. They shake the whole bloody glacier.

I am trying to free myself. The rope is coming loose.

The Commander's address has not gone down well. He and his assistant enter the tent. In the corner there is a jerrycan of kerosene. I try to shout. Words don't come out. The Commander douses himself with kerosene. The other assistants do the same. Don't do it, I try to beg them, convulsing in my chair. The Commander strikes a match and sets himself and the assistants on fire. Bloody bastards, I realize: they have changed the *plan*; they were going to untie our ropes and hand themselves in. Fire was not part of the plan. I struggle. I scream. My hands break free. The flames are spreading. I leap towards the captives and untie their ropes. The General runs with the Defense Minister out of the tent. What have you done, Chef? I scream. The storm troopers start shooting. The General shouts: Do not shoot! The troopers enter the tent, followed by the colonel, who tries to drag me out. I resist. The plates fall down. He overpowers me. The last thing I hear is loud barking of a dog.

There is a helicopter waiting. Rotors running. The colonel rushes the General and the Minister and me to the Cheetah helicopter.

From the air we see flames and smoke and troops scattering. The wind is so severe it separates the tent into two. From the air we see two little oranges, one on the Indian side and the other rolling towards the Pakistani side of the glacier.

The smell of burning skin never really leaves you, I say to myself on this train.

21

Is it possible to cook well when one is completely sad? Or when one is completely happy? I ask myself. In our country where half of the children are malnourished, and cannot even read and write, is it all right for some people to eat well? I close my eyes trying to answer, but all I see are the shadows. The shadow of Chef Kishen in the kitchen, and the shadow of General Sahib on the carpets, and the soldiers on the glacier. My eyes ache when I think about the glacier. The sun is out. The sky is cobalt blue. Blue is too bright for me.

My head is aching. My brain is. Am I already dead?

India keeps passing by.

Outside, the land is impoverished, not planted. No river, only a polluted stream. The land is parched and yellow and flat with an occasional rise, then flat again. Flatness is terrifying. An occasional animal flashes by. A defecating man or woman flash by. The town of Pathankot passes by. Troops and tanks go by. Now the foothills are visible. Distant mountains, the Pir Panjals, are visible. Now we are far away from the Delhis and Bombays. Far away from the maximum cities, far away from a million people and their miseries, and a hazaar million melancholies. Kashmir is close by. I can smell it. Akhni. Yakhni. The *mehek* of saffron. The beauty. The sadness of mountains. The disquiet of plane trees. The accumulation of snow. Large flakes and powder fallen on cobbled streets. In winter all streets look alike, all houses alike. Snow is whirling in the air. Smoke rises from the braziers. Embers in wicker kangris. Beauty, I am coming. I am on my way. I have not forgotten your fragile pastries. The ridges on your leavened bread. Half-eaten pomegranate in General Sahib's fridge. Cherries so big they redden Rubiya's hands, Irem's fingers. Kashmir, you are *real*. You are my half-chilled soup, minced cilantro, my zaman pilaf. Bittersweat chukunder. Rista. Aab gosht. Gurdé Kaporé. Kidney and testicle curry. Kaléji. Sheermal. Lavasa. Tsot. Maythi paratha. Kabuli chana. Nargissi kebab. Tamatar muli. You are a sudden red mirchi. You give me pleasure and pain, both at once. You are my dream, my desire. My North, my Brain. My pounding headache. You are my weed, my cancer. My egg yolk.

You are colder than death, colder than love. *Kaschemir. Cashmere. Qashmir. Cachemire.*

Cushmeer. Casmir. Kerseymere. Koshmar.
I can smell you. Paradise.
Ice.
Paradice.
I can't see a thing.
Did I dream a glacier?
Am I dead?
What am I doing here? Minutes ago I woke up in this air-conditioned bogie. The windows are double-glazed.

'What am I doing here?' I ask the khaki-clad man. 'Why on earth am I in this carriage? I was traveling second-class. What happened?'

'Sahib, around 10 o'clock, three or four hours ago, you had stepped into the bathroom of that second-class bogie you were traveling in.'

'Yes, yes.'

'You passed out in the bathroom, Sahib.'

'I collapsed?'

I look down. My hands are dirty.

'Seizure, Sahib. Fortunately there was a doctor in the bogie. On his recommendation, we the railway staff moved you on a stretcher to this air-conditioned bogie.'

'Shookriya,' I say. 'Thank you. I must pay for the extra ticket.'

Some people who work for the Railways are exceptionally kind. I am not talking about the corrupt TT's and the crook Ministers, but workers like this attendant. He is one of those rare people who do not expect a tip. Just like soldiers in the army.

'No, Sahib. I will not accept extra money.'

'But you must. I insist.'

'Don't worry, Sahib. You served in the army.'

'How do you know I served?'

'The whole train knows *you served*. News travels fast on trains, Sahib.'

Even on trains there is no privacy, I say to myself.

'Has the train *covered* time?' I ask. 'If it does not *cover*, I will miss the bus.'

How and when they moved my body and luggage to this compartment, I have no recall. He is the first man on the train I feel like talking to. The man is wearing a khaki uniform. Says he used to work as a lineman. The Railways made me a lineman. For thirty-one years I worked as a lineman. For thirty-one years I was unhappy. But when I started growing old the Railways transferred me inside the train, Sahib. We were so overworked, he said, sometimes on two hours of sleep we changed the lines, gave signals, and it was a lot of responsibility. So many lives depended on me. I could not imagine making a mistake, Sahib. Making even one would equal mass murder.

The air inside the bogie is refreshingly cold. From very hot I have moved to very cold. I do not say this to him. Instead I ask the attendant for a blanket. When he returns with my blanket I ask: Now that you work inside the train, are you not worried that some other lineman on two hours of sleep might make the same mistake you feared the most?

'No, Sahib, it will not be my mistake. Working inside the train is much better than the duty of a lineman outside.'

'So, you are not afraid that you might die?'

'If I think about death all the time, I will not be able to work, Sahib. Now if you will please allow me.'

He disappears to his cabin (as I found out later) to play cards with the second attendant.

I hear the hum of air-conditioning, and many foreign accents, in this bogie. From my berth I can see two foreign women, dressed in Indian salwar-kameez. The more they try to look like Indians, the more they stand out. The women are quite fair and beautiful. One has blue eyes.

First: Canadian?

Second: No. From Texas.

First: But you carry a Canadian flag on your bag?

Second: The American flag lands me in trouble.

First: My name is Veronica. I am from Mexico City.

Second: Willow from Texas. From across the border!

They shake hands.

One of them says: *The only bloody thing in India on time was the train.*

Who said it? Willow or Veronica?

My head is pounding. My body is shivering. I beckon the attendant.

'Please, it is very cold,' I say to the man.

Not as a complaint, but by way of making a simple request.

'The temperature is pre-set, Sahib.'

'Can you do something about the noise at least? I have a bad headache.'

'AC makes a lot of noise, these coaches are old, Sahib. This one is from the time of the British. The air-conditioning was installed where the iceboxes used to be in these bogies. Those days the compartments were kept cold by using blocks of ice, Sahib. When the train stopped at big junctions, coolies standing on platforms would transfer ice to the boxes, sahib.'

'Please, my head is pounding.'

Willow and Veronica are both carrying cell phones. They seem to have developed a quick friendship. I don't know who took more initiative. Willow or Veronica, or maybe both?

They laugh a lot. At first I thought they were laughing at the poverty of our country. I was wrong. Laughing was basically a way to forget all the difficulties they were encountering dealing with the civilians in our country. They laughed a lot about toilets and latrines.

Just to hear them has made me feel young again. I am not dying, I say to myself.

Tuh-dee Tuh-dee Tuh-deeee Tuh-deeee
Tuh-dee Tuh-dee Tuh-deeee Tuh-deeee

Catering-wallah comes into our bogie. The women order hard-boiled eggs. He says he has no more eggs left. I have potato cutlets only, he says. They buy the cutlets. Too bad you don't have eggs, I demand. And the man smiles and produces a perfect hard-boiled egg.

'You did not sell the girls the eggs?' I ask.

'Sahib, I have only one egg, and they are two. I could not choose who gets the egg, so I decided not to give either one of them the egg.'

One girl makes eye contact with me. I translate from Hindi to English. I tell her the catering-wallah's exact reasoning, and the moment I finish they break into a fit of laughter.

'Where in India are you from?' asks one of them.

231

I am at a loss for words.

'Not an Indian,' I say. 'Brazilian.'

Then silence.

Aren't they nice, my shoes. They will outlast me. They will continue to live. They will not be cremated. I do not want to be cremated. There is nothing sacred about fire. I have no fondness for burials either. I like the towers of silence. The Parsees leave the bodies of the dead for the vultures. The birds eat while flying, one is neither on this earth, nor in the heavens yet. Sometimes a limb falls on ground from the beak of a flying bird and worms on earth feel graced, a river or a jungle gets nourished.

What will happen the day I die?

Clouds will collide with mountain tops. Thunder. Then nothing.

Once gone, I do not want to return to this earth. No more reincarnations.

Five or six of us had an audience with His Holiness in Dharamshala, Willow tells Veronica. The *Dali Lama* told us a story. (She meant Dalai Lama, but she pronounced *Dali Lama*.) A monk who served eighteen years in a Chinese gulag was finally released under the condition that he would not return to Tibet. When the Lama first met him, the monk said that he was in great danger and several times he didn't think he would make it. The Lama asked him what kind of danger was he in? The monk replied that he was in great danger of losing compassion towards the Chinese.

Good story, says Veronica.

I urge you to please replace China with America and Tibet with Iraq. There is a real danger, Veronica. Danger of losing compassion towards the Americans.

This time the women did not laugh.

When people talk religion and politics, I turn my thoughts to food. The catering-wallah's egg is over-boiled. It has the odor of sulphur. The pleasures of eating food cooked by others! I can't eat this egg. I will throw it away. No food is better than bad food. But.

The girl-woman is beautiful.

Willow or Veronica?

Maybe both.

They disappear to the toilet for a while; one returns in an oversize red T-shirt. No. 1 International Terrorist — it is written on the T-shirt. Under the writing is a photo of a face which resembles the American President.

The girls start laughing again. I feel very tired. Their laughter reminds me of the bleak laughter of the Kashmiri people. They are real jokers, the Kashmiris. I hear them everywhere. Impossible to escape them. The Kashmiri laughter wounds me wherever I go. Kashmir was a beautiful place and we have made a bloody mess of it. Will the Kashmiris, too, lose compassion for us Indians? I ask myself. Will I lose compassion towards certain people?

There are, and there were, people who occupied my mind all the time — and they ruined me. They made me what I am today, and I bow before them, and am thankful, but, it is certain, these people have also managed to ruin me. They had a weakness for giving commands and I had a weakness for accepting them more or less. Sometimes just to please them I would do whatever they felt like doing and I would pretend I liked whatever they liked. Chef used to go biking and I would say I too like biking but really if I could help it I would have slept longer, there was so little time to sleep in the army.

I wish I had a mind of my own, a free mind. I wish I had led a life separate from influence. I was like a child, and my fingers were in the hands of two or three important people and they pulled me this way or that.

After Chef died I did not read the papers for a while. But when I did, there was no story about him anyway. He died for a big nothing. There was nothing on TV. The press and the media had reported nothing to the nation. That is why I think in the larger scheme of things the man died for one big nothing.

On the other hand there were reports

about the colonel who had staged fake battles on the glacier, and filmed them, to get a gallantry medal. The papers were also filled with ongoing talk about the coffin scam. But there was no mention of Kishen. The government censored the story. Chef's fate was similar to the fate of the Pakistani troops and officers who died in the war. Pakistan had sent them to India posed as *freedom fighters*, and when they died Pakistan did not even acknowledge them as dead soldiers. Muslim troops in our regiments buried the dead Pakistani soldiers, because the enemy army refused to accept the bodies back. Pakistan maintained a fiction. They had to. And what Chef said that morning during his address on the glacier was the truth, but we had to maintain the lie. In the barracks rumors flowed like rum. But after his first suicide attempt, people started saying they did not know him at all. Those who had consumed his delicacies started saying Kishen? Who is Kishen? He was the most serious and sincere of us all. But he was dead. Not a single watch lost a second in our country. This country produced him. This miserable, melancholic, cowdungofacountry produced him. Then *it* took him away. He did not kill himself. *It* killed him.

Now this is killing me.

The reason I wanted to read the papers and watch TV was to find out how his parents and loved ones had responded. Not to get the details I already knew, but to find out about his family. I walked to the hospital, and I saw the nurse in white. She was always in white, but that day the color took special significance.

She knew he was gone. And she was expecting me. She asked me if Chef had mentioned her.

I did not respond.

She wept. She held my arm and wept.

'He talked about you a lot,' I said. 'He only talked about you.'

'Was the fire an accident?' she asked.

'Yes,' I lied, 'it was a kitchen accident.'

'What a way to die,' she said.

She was grieving him. But I do not think anyone should grieve him. For once he did exactly what he felt like doing. He had designed the complete menu. It was a perfect glacier meal. Chef dared to question the universe.

He questioned the Siachen coffin scam and the ration scam, which ran into five thousand crore millions of rupees, I didn't tell her. The colonel, the brigadier, the major general and other senior officers involved in the scams were not even charged. Instead they received early retirement with full pension and benefits. Now they run big hotels and malls, and reside in fashionable glass towers and drive yellow Hummers. Two or three represent our country in foreign lands as ambassadors. Isn't this the biggest shame on this earth that the man who wanted to improve the army is forgotten, not even acknowledged, and the men who destroyed it every month receive fat pension checks and benefits? Why was I born in this country?

The cancer that has grown inside me is not my fault. This country caused it. Despite that it has no shame. There are voices inside me, voices of people close to me, and they keep saying that I am personally responsible for bringing the disease and illness on myself. But it is not my fault at all.

I walked to the ladies ward. There was no one inside. Normally when Irem was not there, her shoes or at least her few belongings were visible under the metal bed. Now the ward was empty. I stood by Irem's bed. Her name and number were gone and insects were climbing the wall. The nurse told me that the captive had been moved elsewhere.

'Where?'

She did not know.

'They are looking for you.'

'For me?'

'You must report at the colonel's office.'

There was a fog and I followed the gravel road to the khaki office building. The colonel was alone in the room, so I did not have to wait long. His office orderly announced me, and although the colonel didn't look up I marched in anyway. His cap was lying on his desk, and he was reading a thick file.

'Jai Hind, sir,' I said.

No response.

I noticed the circles left on his desk by cups of chai and coffee.

I coughed.

Suddenly he raised his head, stared at me and snapped his fingers and asked the office orderly to bring the *thing*. I noticed the colonel's trussed jacket, his curly hair. Coconut oil glistened on the curls.

The orderly unlocked the Godrej almirah in the room, and pulled out the *thing*.

'Play it.'

The orderly played my tape recorder.

'We confiscated this from the enemy woman in the hospital ward,' said the colonel.

'Sir.'

'You gave the enemy woman this American music?'

'German music, sir.'

'Yes, yes, I know. The enemy played it again and again for two full days — very loud

— this music. Why did you give it to her?'

'Sir, I thought, sir, music would ease the tension. General Sahib had asked me, sir, to conduct interrogations delicately, sir.'

'The interrogations are over, Kirpal.'

'Sir.'

'This was a serious breach of order, Kirpal. I am giving you the last warning. General Kumar knew your Father Sahib. I knew him too. He was our finest officer. You have been pardoned because of your father. This must never happen again. Understand?'

Then he buried his face in the file again. I looked at the tea and coffee circles on the desk, and his cap. After a while I coughed.

'You are still here?'

'Sir, where is the woman sir?'

'Woman?'

'The enemy woman, sir?'

'Not here.'

'Sir.'

'Dismiss.'

★   ★   ★

I now know the name of the music she heard. Chef Kishen had received that tape from Chef Muller in the German embassy during his training, but he did not know the title of the music. For many years I did not know the title either. It was only last year I found out. I visited the German embassy in Delhi. The yellow-haired girl at the embassy sent me to Goethe House, where the music librarian asked me to sing that piece of music.

I tried.

TUH-dee TUH-dee
TA-deeee TA-deeee
TUH-dee TUH-dee
TA-deeee TA-deeee

'Try again,' she said.

Daam Dum De-daaam De-daaam
Daam Dum De-daaam De-daaam

'One more time,' she said.
'This one goes slowly,' I said.

Daaah Daaah Da Daaah It Vit
Daaah Daaah Da Daaah It Vit

'More,' she said.
'The tune is almost a military march,' I said.

TUH-dee TUH-dee TA-deeee TA-deeee
TUH-dee TUH-dee TA-deeee TA-deeee

'This sounds Turkish to me,' she said. 'There is no such thing. In German tradition there is no such thing.'

'But, I have heard the music,' I said.

My hands moved up in the air, then down and up again. I found myself conducting — just like Chef Kishen had done on the glacier — as I sang or tried to sing that music.

Da Da Da Da
Da Da Da Da
Da Da Da Da
Deee da Daaa

'The Ninth.' She jumped from her seat.

'The Ninth?'

'Beethoven,' she said.

'Bay-toh-behn?'

'Beethoven,' she said.

'Beethoven.'

'Yes.'

'He wrote that music just like that?' I asked.

'No,' she said. 'It took him thirty years to write it. He made many errors. But, finally he found perfection.'

She gave me a headset and I listened to the complete Ninth at the booth. She told me where to buy works by Beethoven.

'But I am only interested in the Ninth,' I answered.

'Maybe.'

She gave me a book, so I read it. The man was completely deaf when he wrote that piece of music. *Tuh-dee Tuh-dee Ta-deeee Ta-deeee.* I simply could not believe it. It is like a cook who can't smell or taste trying to create a new dish to make millions of people happy. *Tuh-dee Tuh-dee Ta-deeee Ta-deeee.* This has stayed with me all these years. The Ninth has stayed. It is not just music. It is *real*. My whole wretched life is embedded in it. And I do not care if it comes from Germany. I am dying, but I have heard the music. My fear, my fury, my joy, my melancholy — everything is embedded in this piece. The Ninth is *real*. It penetrates my body like smells, like food. And yet: it is *solid* and massive like a glacier. Shifting. Sliding. Melting. Then becoming air. When I listen to this music so many places penetrate me. So many times. So many sounds. Voices. The voices do a tamasha, and I am able to say it for the first time. The Ninth is *real*. It is the kiss, the most powerful and delicate kissforthewholeworld.

Da   Da   Da   Da
Da   Da   Da   Da
Da   Da   Da   Da
Deee   Da   Daaa

22

In November General Sahib was approved by Delhi to become the next Governor of Kashmir. Sahib was a good choice for the post. He was the 'Hero of Kargil' and the 'Hero of Siachen Glacier'. The State needed urgently a gentleman-soldier at the very top to restore order. Sahib arranged to take me (and the gardener Agha) along to the Raj Bhavan, his new residence in Srinagar. It was a rare honor. Kishen would have been proud to see me occupy the highest kitchen in Kashmir.

On the night of his appointment General Kumar delivered a speech on radio and TV.

My fellow Indians,
This troubled and beautiful land is ready for peace. Our task is not going to be easy, many challenges lie ahead, but together we will find a solution. In my opinion the first thing we must tackle is the question of governance and power. How will I, as your administrator, use power? Let me reassure you that I will act in an enlightened, just, and humane way. I will lead by reason and

cooperation and set an example not just for the poor countries, but also for the rich ... Thomas Jefferson once said, let me quote: 'The less power we use the greater it will be.' I convey my warm greetings to all of you and wish you peace and prosperity. Jai Hind.

This speech made a great impression on me. Those first few days I worked even harder to please Gen Sahib. One day he asked me especially to cater the wedding banquet for the preceding Governor's daughter. Her name was Bina. The girl was stunningly beautiful and well-educated. She had spent years in London and New York and was getting married to an Indian boy who had also spent time in New York and London. Both had moved back *home* because they did not want to be treated *second class* in those foreign lands. Bina took great interest in Indian art, buildings and food. She had even gotten involved with the Department of Tourism to write glossy brochures for foreign visitors. She handed me, during our second meeting, a brochure she had written herself about the Governor's residence.

More than anything else I remember the smell of wood inside the Raj Bhavan. The richly decorated papier-mâché ceilings. The fifty-five rooms. Dimly lit corridors. Red curtains. Crystal chandeliers. It was easy to get lost in the labyrinths of the building. The interiors were done entirely in walnut and deodar and rose, and the kitchen was large, airy, always filled with light. From the west window it was possible to see the ruins of the Mughal garden on the slopes of the mountain, also General Sahib's old residence.

Bina's tourist brochure was an elegant piece of work, and whenever I try to describe that residence I bring it to mind. For me describing buildings is harder than detecting the ingredients in an exotic dish and certainly more difficult than describing human faces. People hide their true selves behind a face, but buildings hide even more. The Raj Bhavan, Bina had written, is perched on the beautiful Zabarwan hill and quivers with the fragrance of crocuses, and irises, and narcissi. The steep road to the compound is lined by majestic plane trees (also known as *bouin* or *chenar*). The mansion commands a stunning view of the Dal Lake, the ancient ruins, the snow-clad mountain ranges, and the Hazrat-bal Mosque. On the east side is a large cherry orchard, and on the west the Royal Springs Golf Course.

* * *

245

The banquet, I must say, was my best accomplishment to this date. We had a pre-banquet dinner as well, which I cooked on a small scale for eight chosen guests — the old Governor and his daughter met me before the dinner to decide the menu and I had to use some tact to convey that most of their choices were simply wrong, and whenever the old Governor started insisting on a dish, Bina (like Rubiya) would wink her eye and smile as if saying to me, just ignore him, he is being fussy for nothing.

Bina took me aside and said if I could give the banquet a *paisley* theme she would do anything for me. I did not know what *paisley* was, and she told me that it was the pattern on the blouse she was wearing. You mean that tear-shaped thing? I asked. It is also a comma, she said. It can be seen as a mango. It can be many things. Touch it, she said. You mean you want me to touch your blouse? Yes, she said. Is this silk? I asked. It was very soft. She said it was different from the silk people bought in showrooms. This is called *peace silk*. This silk is made without killing the silkworms.

In the kitchen I thought about *paisley* for a long time, and thanks to Bina I finally found out the name for the embroidery I had seen on Irem's pheran. Her pheran had paisley all over, not just on the borders.

The ruins of the Mughal garden, as I said before, were visible from the kitchen window, and they, too, for some unknown reason (in my mind) became associated with paisley. Sometimes wild animals appeared in the upper terraces and made strange sounds. While cooking I would ask, How is it possible for such beauty and such extreme forms of cruelty to co-exist? I would think about the beauty of the gardens in Kashmir and the Mughals who had built them. The Emperors were such learned men, scholars they were, they kept journals and ate good food. They took cuisine to perfection. They took architecture to perfection. They built the Taj, and yet how cruel they were. Not just cruel to others, but son to father, and brother to brother. How could these two things co-exist in the same person, in the same kingdom, and I felt there must be something wrong about Chef Muller's theory. Muller had told Kishen that it was possible to identify the qualities of a person from what they ate. How can people who eat the finest delicacies commit the most horrible crimes? I would ask myself.

Two days before the banquet, a curfew was imposed on the city because of militant violence. Bombs and IE devices exploded in downtown. I needed prawns and fish and

247

ingredients for cioppino — the Italian soup — and many other things. Bina was nervous, but the captain who escorted me into the city told her not to worry. He ordered the pilot jeep to accompany the Governor's black car, in which I sat on the front seat, and my two assistants sat on the back, and two military trucks moved ahead of the car and two moved behind, and a windowless armored vehicle raced on the side, and that is how I went to the bazaar to shop for the banquet. The shops were closed because of the curfew, so we knocked and woke up the shopkeepers one by one, and I told them not to worry because we meant no harm, and if they refused to charge I paid them anyway.

On the wedding day the Prime Minister himself flew to the Raj Bhavan, and the Defense Minister was also present along with other high dignitaries and eminent personalities. General Chibber, General Raina, Shri Bhagat, Mr Modi and Dr Jagdish Tytler. Colonel Chowdhry and Patsy Memsahib. The white American ambassador and his black secretary and the chief of the World Bank. Business tycoons. Only government journalists were allowed, the event was not announced to the public, and after the meal the Prime Minister demanded that I show my face, and I appeared in a liveried dress meant for special occasions. I walked straight to the drawing room, somewhat nervous, but the PM put me at ease by telling a Sikh joke, and we all laughed.

'Well done, Kirpal ji,' he said. 'One day when Governor Sahib is not around, we will have to steal you!'

Later many guests recited poetry, and the Prime Minister recited his own poems, and a bureaucrat translated, and the PM said that it was the most perfect translation of his poems from Hindi into English, and the foreign guests applauded with loud clapping. Sahib opened the most expensive French wine to *honor poetry*, and the more he drank the more the PM changed and looked different from his photos in magazines.

It was a grand affair. Because the number of guests was over three hundred, we had to set up a special scullery tent in the area close to the servants' quarters. We hired temporary staff. We had to get security clearance for all of them — whether they were Muslims or non-Muslims, but mostly they were poor Muslims. We managed to sneak most of them in without the clearance. There were around a hundred waiting staff.

Golf-ball-sized goshtaba. Tails of sheep. Paisley-shaped naans. Moorish eggplant. Murgh Wagah. Rogan Josh. Pasta with roasted chestnuts and walnuts. Paella valenciana. Pavlova salad. Oysters. I remember it fresh like yesterday. The bartender came from Bombay (with his special English brandy). Bollywood stars flew in. Red carpets lined the walkways. Red shamiana tents were pitched under chenar trees. The Hindu priest had a PhD in Sanskrit. Bina changed her dress thirteen times. She and the groom circled the fire seven times. The air smelled of an epic wedding, flowers everywhere. Columns and spheres and disks and mandalas of pansies and marigolds and jasmines and daffodils and roses. Wild roses. The kitchen door was open and I heard footsteps. From behind the curtains I saw the outgoing Governor, in profile, and the incoming Governor guiding the special guests to the glass cabinet in the drawing room. General Sahib pointed at the famous photo from the '71 India-Pakistan War.

In the photo General Aurora of our army is sitting next to General Niazi of the Pakistani army. The Pakistani defeat is very fresh. India has taken 90,000 Pakistani soldiers into captivity. General Niazi is signing the surrender documents.

'I was present during the surrender, sir,' said General Kumar Sahib. 'Gen Niazi looked absolutely humiliated.'

'Kumar Sahib, what happened right after the surrender?' inquired the PM.

'Gen Niazi removed his rank, sir, and emptied his pistol, and he handed the pistol to our victorious Gen Aurora.'

'But how did the pistol end up here?' The PM demanded an explanation.

'Gen Aurora made me the custodian of the pistol, sir. This is still a very reliable firearm!'

'Reliable or not,' said the PM seriously, 'this pistol must go to the War Museum in Delhi.'

The General laughed mildly, and opened the glass cabinet and the pistol passed through several hands.

Holding the pistol, the PM said: 'Wherever *they* are there is trouble.'

'But we know the reliable way to contain *them*, sir,' said the old Governor.

'People of Kashmir are unhappy with Delhi, sir,' said General Sahib, the new Governor.

'Well, we are unhappy with them too!' said the PM.

Then they all laughed.

Single malt was served on the rocks.

Finally I could no longer see their faces. Bloody bastard, I said. The dessert is still not ready. Bina was a bit worried about my ability to tackle Italian desserts, but I reassured her.

She approved my suggestion to serve tiramisu at the banquet.

'Sculpt it like paisley!' she reminded me just outside the scullery tent.

'Bina,' I said, 'this is an excellent way to make the Italian mithai our own! Bina, please don't worry. I will make you happy. I will make all the three hundred guests extremely happy. Chef Kishen taught me the most authentic recipe from Florence, Tus-canny.'

'You mean Tuscany?'

'I think so.'

The night before I had started looking for bottles of rum. Rum is one of the most essential ingredients. You can do without vanilla, you can do without cinnamon, but you can't do without rum in tiramisu. Cocoa, coffee, cream, sponge fingers, mascarpone cheese, eggs, sugar, and rum. The old servant told me that the bottles were stored in the corner room in the Raj Bhavan, and it took me a while to find the right room in those labyrinths, but I did find it finally, and after procuring two bottles I drank a big burra-peg, standing underneath a big chande-lier, to deal with the stress and hard work, and then, I do not know how, I lost my way in the building, and found myself going down the stairs and up the stairs, clutching a bottle, and down again to a room with worn furniture and faded wallpaper and carpets and thin walls. I think it was around two o'clock in the morning. Voices were coming from the neighboring room. It was as if two people were having a good time. Through a little hole in the wall I peeked in and saw a figure who resembled the outgoing Governor's son. I do not remember his name, in my mind he is Bina's brother. He was with a girl in that room. I half-finished the bottle and kept looking through the hole. The girl was very fair. Kashmiri girls are always very fair. But. There were dark marks under her eyes. She was giving him a blowjob. After some time he spread his semen on her fair skin and milk-white breasts. She had huge aureoles. Her hair was wild. But she did not seem to be liking it. When he was done he opened the door. As she followed him, he said, I will live up to my promise, you whore, I always live up to my promise. I did not do this to you for nothing, he said, and I hid behind a crate, unable to follow them, scared because I knew the whole area was under heavy surveillance, and there were loaded guns. Please release my brother, I heard the woman's voice say. Let her out, Bina's brother ordered the sentry. I went back to my room and swallowed two more mouthfuls of rum.

After the wedding and the banquet Bina

(now Mrs Ramani) left with her husband to honeymoon in Gulmarg. Gulmarg means meadow-of-flowers in Kashmiri. Her parents kissed her goodbye, and so did her brother. She was wearing a blue peace silk with paisley and of course she looked very beautiful. She thanked me by planting a kiss on my cheek. She recommended to her father, the ex-Governor, that I be sent on a well-deserved holiday to my home to be with my *people*. At that point I could not ask for anything better.

23

I am such a pea.

I don't like *mutters*.

Mutter-paneer, mutter-aloo, mutter-gobi.

There is a small area the size of a pea in our brains. I read it in the paper. This area is just behind the eye. Compassion and empathy lie in this area. When the area gets damaged we torture others more easily, and with less mess to ourselves.

In Delhi, while on leave, I could not stop thinking of Kashmir. I would shut my eyes or try distracting myself, but the more I tried the more forcefully the images flashed before me.

When will you get married? Mother would ask, and the question would annoy and sadden me. All my uncles and aunties wanted to hear were tales about the *heroism* of our soldiers at the border, and I found the June heat unbearable, and the June mosquitoes unbearable at night. Images of mountains and mosques and Raj Bhavan disturbed my sleep. Sometimes I would think about Irem. Sometimes the beauty of the valley and Sufi music filled my dreams. I would see Kashmiri women in pherans pounding dried red chilies. I cut short my holiday and returned on this very train.

★ ★ ★

Srinagar had become a war zone during my absence.

The streets trembled with armored vehicles.

Militancy was at its peak again.

The enemy was training more men and brainwashing more boys, and wave after wave crossed into Kashmir to set off bombs at public places, even inside army camps. Fifty new battalions were raised by our army to contain the insurgents. For every four civilians we had one soldier. But things were going badly. During those dark days no one on the General's staff was a Muslim. The only Muslim in the Raj Bhavan was the old gardener, Agha.

★ ★ ★

Nothing is ready. Nothing.

It is early, no fire in the kitchen yet. I am still planning the day. There is a knock. I see a wrinkled hand. The rear door opens. Agha, the gardener, is standing in front of me. Teeth gone. Skullcap on head, three-day stubble like

256

a dusting of snow. A rag of a sash around his neck.

As usual he doesn't step in.

'Do you have something to polish this with?' he asks.

He is holding an old fountain nozzle. The metal is layered with green patina.

'Come in,' I say. 'It is getting cold.'

To my surprise he starts removing his shoes.

'You can keep them on.'

He ignores me and walks in bare feet. The kitchen floor is so cold he is standing on the tips of his toes.

'No Problem,' he says.

'This might work,' I say, handing him the bottle of acid I normally use to polish the sink.

'Good,' he says and picks up an old rag and starts work on the nozzle.

His presence makes me uneasy. He keeps muttering poetry while polishing.

'Now you may leave,' I say.

'No Problem,' he says.

He does not leave.

'Do you have a minute?' he asks.

'It has to be quick,' I say.

'Why did you remove your turban?' he asks.

'Yes,' I say. 'My hair is short now.'

'What will your father say?'

'He is dead, Agha. He is buried in the glacier.'

The gardener stops polishing.

'Fathers never die,' he says.

I lift my hand to my face. The beard is gone now, my cheeks are smooth. The turban is no longer on my head, but I sense its weight. It was a big part of me and I removed it. I look at my hands. All the muscles of my hands. The pores of my skin. The tips of my thumb and middle finger. The whorls, the roughness, the cuts. My hands are freezing. They start shaking. I strike a match. It doesn't work. Agha helps me light up the stove.

'Do you still have a minute?' he asks.

He has no patience.

'Please be quick,' I say.

'No Problem,' he says.

'Yes, yes, be quick.'

'My son disappeared two days ago.'

'He will come back,' I say.

'No,' he says.

'Did he become a militant?' I ask.

'He simply disappeared.'

'Sorry, I must get back to work.'

The nozzle is shining now, reflecting Agha's face.

'No Problem,' he says and walks slowly to his old shoes and shuts the door behind him. A cold draft hits my cheeks.

Later in the evening when I am done with the dinner I spot him sitting by the marigolds in the garden, smoking a hookah. His breath stinks of nicotine.

'No Problem,' he says.

He looks more dead than alive.

'What do you mean?' I say. 'Your son.'

'He is gone.'

'No, no. But how do you really feel? Not just about your son, but the situation in Kashmir?'

'Bad things are expected during the *turmoil*,' he says. 'Why should the most beautiful place on earth be spared bad things? People are turning mad here. This place is becoming a pagal-khana, a lunatic asylum.'

'Where do you suspect your son is?'

'They should *stop* torturing our boys,' he says.

'They?'

'Military,' he says.

'Where?'

'In the hotels,' he says.

'You are a joker, Agha,' I say.

'No Problem,' he says.

★ ★ ★

His words disturbed me a lot. I found it difficult to cook. Difficult to sleep. It was true. Our army had occupied many hotels in Srinagar. But they were the new residences for our officers and jawans, I had not imagined them as sites of torture. I decided to visit. Part of me wanted to disprove Agha. Barring a few bad apples our army was basically good. The only way it was possible for me to access the hotels was by taking extra initiative. General Sahib was pleased by my proposal, and he granted me the permission to inspect kitchens in all the army-occupied hotels. I became a part-time inspector of kitchens.

Hotel Athena. Hotel Duke. Hotel Nedou. Oberoi Palace. More than thirty-six hotels now belonged to the army. Before inspection, I would read the tourism department's write-up for that particular site, then a special vehicle would take me to the hotel (cycling was no longer safe) and I would arrive unannounced just before meals and taste the food and inspect the kitchen hygiene, and then excuse myself for a few minutes, and during that brief time I would hurriedly check the rooms.

Agha was wrong.

Our army was out shooting films. Everything was being done in the open, there was nothing to hide, the rooms were clean, certain scenes were being shot inside the hotels, others outdoors. Light. The most important ingredient in cinema is light. One needs the right kind of light to screen a film, just like one needs the right kind of light to shoot a film. (I remember, in Grade 3, I watched a film shot in Kashmir. The hero fought the villains first in the Mughal garden, then in the colonial-style hotel with red shingles. There was something magical about the quality of light in Kashmir.) Because of the new assignment I witnessed the shootings of many films. I was able to understand the connections between light and cinema. I was also able to compare the art of filmmaking with the art of cooking. A dish does not last more than a meal, but a film is for ever. Some people give up eating meat after watching the slaughter of a goat. But no one gives up the movies after witnessing a shooting.

If I were asked to give a collective title to all the films our army was shooting in the hotels, it will be called *Masters of Light* or *Colonel Madhok's Diary of a Bad Year*. There was a scene which involved a man tied with a rope to an iron pillar. A captain shoved a cricket bat up the man's anus. Light was warm and soft in the room. There was a boy crawling like an infant in a pool of his own

261

shit and urine. There were naked men in the semi-darkness of sparkling Diwali lights. Two or three German shepherds snarled at their privates, men's penises squirming. In Hotel Nedou I discovered men standing under light so harsh and bright it burned their skin, and a machine kept emitting sounds like *ping, ping, ping* while giving shocks to the testicles of a Kashmiri tied to a wet mattress. In Hotel Athena I found hair and nipples and electrodes in cold outdoor light. Downstairs, close-up of a detached hand in underexposed light. Blackout. Pigs. Blood. Semen. In Oberoi Palace four male nurses were force-feeding two men in the fading light of the evening. There were tubes stuck up their noses and into their throats. But, I was not looking for men.

Only one person.

Irem.

From the tourist department I got a list of all the hotels in the valley, and finally I visited every single one, but I failed to find her.

Then something else happened. Sahib did not go for his morning walk that day because of light rain. When the rain stopped Sahib stepped out and sat on the bench in the garden. He ordered tea. Through the open kitchen window I observed everything.

The ayah took the tea tray and the daily

paper to the garden. I had added ginger in the tea. Normally I would add a clove and crushed cardamom, but that morning I added ginger as well.

Sahib motioned with his hand, as if to say, leave the tray on the bench.

She planted the tray and placed a roll of paper between the tray and Sahib's crossed legs. He unfolded the *Times*.

'Please ask Agha to see me.'

She walked to the edge and beckoned the man raking the leaves in the garden. Not far from the yellow pile his transistor radio was playing rag malar. He stopped and literally ran to the bench.

'Salaam, Sahib.'

'Agha, how is the garden?'

'The begonias have bloomed, Sahib, and the faulty fountain nozzle has been repaired, but it is no longer like the old one.'

'Something more important?'

The gardener's canvas shoes dropped a cake of mud as he shifted on green, neatly trimmed grass. He kept his eyes downcast.

'Your son is dead, Agha,' General Sahib raised his voice. Sahib rarely raised his voice.

The gardener remained still.

'Do you hear me?'

The gardener still didn't move.

'You didn't even tell?'

263

Agha held his face between his hands.

'Show him the paper.' Sahib turned to the ayah. 'He can't read, but he knows the photo.'

Agha studied the front page.

'Look at your son. Is he in heaven now? Overnight he made you the father of a martyr. Thirty-seven people inside the bus terminal, Agha — all Kashmiris.'

'My son DEAD, Sahib.'

'The bus was to leave for Pakistani Kashmir. Fifty-six miles after fifty-six years. Fifty-six wasted years, Agha. And your son plants a bomb. Shabash.'

'Passenger not hurt, Sahib.'

'Passenger not hurt, Sahib,' he mimicked. 'Two majors, just out of the academy, killed. Finish. Khatam.'

'Sahib — '

'From this bench I used to watch your son. Only a few months ago he watered the trees in this garden. But one thing I will not say, I will not say he was misguided. He well knew the consequences.'

The gate opened. The guard posted outside the Raj Bhavan opened it. The nurse from the army hospital entered, and propped her bicycle by the fence. By the time General Sahib looked over his shoulder she had disappeared into the house.

'You were going to lose your pension as

well, Agha. But I have urged the colonel to reconsider.'

'No, Sahib?' He stood up.

'Agha, the army fears for my life. We must let you go.'

'But, Sahib, I am not my son.'

The General stood up. He turned and started beckoning the uniforms. The ADC rushed to the bench.

'Talk to Agha.'

Agha would not leave. Two of the guards forced him to pack his things and threw him out. His feet crushed red and yellow leaves on the narrow path he followed.

The General walked to the gate and looked at the bend in the road for a long time until Agha disappeared.

Later he entered the mansion and climbed the stairs over the kitchen and walked slowly through the dimly lit corridor. In the bedroom he sat in a chair not far from the huge painting on the wall. The dead woman looked down at him from the painting.

I served breakfast in the bedroom.

Porridge. Upma. Papaya.

Orange-pomegranate juice.

Toast with unsalted cheese.

His daughter was lying on the bed. Rubiya was on a special diet. The kitchen had to prepare two separate dishes. One for sir and one for the girl. The nurse examined the girl. Sir moved his chair close to Rubiya and checked her pulse.

'What is my daughter's wish?' he asked.

'Papa,' she said. 'I want to grow up fast.'

'And,' he asked, 'what will *she* become as a grown-up?'

'Emperor,' she said.

'Emperor or Empress?'

'Emperor,' she said.

'His Highness!' He saluted her.

'Papa, I will *kidnap* people!'

'Who will *His Highness* kidnap?'

'You,' she said.

Sahib fell silent for a moment. Then he laughed. Being the Governor was a busy job filled with travel, and certainly the girl felt deprived of his presence. Rubiya was such a lonely child — she used to eat porridge and curds and khitchri, and now she is getting married. I am happy for her.

I am on the train because I am happy for Rubiya.

24

Civ-i-ans. Whatistheword? I am sur-rounded by civilians in this compartment. What presighly is wrong with me? P-r-e-c-i-s-e-l-y? The tumor is in the speech area of your brain, Kip, the doctor explained. Sala asshole.

I can no longer pronounce certain words correctly. But, I can spell them:

R-a-d-i-o.

Yes.

Transformer?

No.

Tranjister?

No.

Spell it.

T-r-a-n-s-i-s-t-e-r.

Days later I found Agha had forgotten his transistor radio in the Raj Bhavan. He had packed his things hurriedly the day he was fired. I found the radio on in the scullery room. Agha was the only Kashmiri on the staff, and no one knew where he lived.

There were food stains on the silver skin of his Philips radio. Agha, you clown, I said, changing thc batteries. The new batteries didn't improve the reception. But, in the slot at the bottom I found a little note scribbled in Kashmiri.

Agha could not read and write. So he must have dictated the lines.

His note led me to the Guest House at the tail end of the Raj Bhavan complex. It used to be the British Resident's summer house, but now served as a lodge for high-ranking guests. The building faced the lake, and it had a proper roof terrace. Agha's note said that the reception will improve on the roof, but it will get better downstairs. Unable to follow the logic, I started climbing down. The reception, as I had expected, became worse and worse. Begum Akhtar was singing ghazals. On the radio her voice sounded like a rejected Indian Idol.

Downstairs was clean. Not a particle of dust. Big portraits of six or seven old Governors looked down from walls as white as snow. I turned off the crackling radio and entered the first room. It was called the Husain Room. The room was devoted entirely to M.F. Husain's paintings of horses. The canvases were huge, twelve feet by eight feet. One almost touched the naked bulb on the wall. I felt dwarfed by the navy-blue and apple-red horses. Reared up on hind legs they looked absolutely alive and stunning. In college the teacher had told us that Husain was the best modern painter in our country, his work was also on display in the National Gallery. No one knows why he is possessed by horses ... He is completely self-taught and his personal life is as eccentric as his art. Husain always walks barefoot, she told us. Did you know? Not only inside the house, but also outside. Even in the hot and bustling streets of Bombay he walks barefoot, and that is exactly how he arrives at the lobbies of five-star hotels and foreign embassies and airports and even English-style clubs. He has all the money in the world to buy hundreds of shoe factories, but he shuns shoes as if foreign objects. Why are you like this? a journalist asked once. When I wear shoes I feel I am eating supper with wrong people, answered the painter.

Standing in front of the horses I removed my shoes and socks. My feet were able to breathe again. I felt connected not only to the painting, but also to the painter. When does a painter know that the painting of a horse is done? I asked myself. In kitchen we are able to tell precisely when a dish is done, but when is the horse *done*? There was something incomplete about the *horses* on the canvas, but it seemed to me that the fragments were *completing* themselves in my head. Cooking is different from painting, I thought. The key ingredients are never absent. Father knew horses . . . when I turned eight he made me feed a horse in the barracks . . . the animal's lips had grabbed the apple swiftly from my hand.

The next room was called the Sher-Gil Hall. Briefly I stood before a dazzling composition, *Two Nudes*. The women looked mysterious despite being naked. However, it did occur to me that the round breasts of the first nude really belonged to the second, and the pointed breasts of the second nude really belonged to the first. The longer I stood there the less I thought about the lips or thighs or breasts, and the more I experienced the warmth and the cold those two women carried inside. They appeared so alone. The reason the painter Husain walks barefoot, I thought, is because he must feel lonely. His art springs out of immense loneliness, I thought.

Diagonally across from the *Two Nudes* were the stunning black and white portraits of musicians, Hari Prasad Chaurasia, the flute player, Zakir Hussein, the tabla player, and Vilayat Khan, the sitar player, and many others. The next room was dark and smelly. No windows. There was a naked bulb hanging from the ceiling on a single wire, and in that dim fragile light I noticed the form of a woman as if sitting on a toilet bowl.

Sorry, I said and stepped out in panic. In the corridor I felt a hand on my shoulder.

'Cook! What are you doing here?'

The guard was armed with a light machine gun.

'Nothing, Major,' I said.

'Nothing?'

'Major,' I explained, 'I was looking for you only. Would you taste the dish I have prepared? Took me fifteen hours of hard work. I offer my new dishes to all the staff members and guards. This is how I learn how good they are!'

'But, why are you carrying your shoes?'

'This place is like a shrine, Major. That is why.'

He looked utterly confused and stared at Agha's radio.

'Here,' I said, handing him the radio. 'Listen to the latest cricket score. Let me bring you the dish.'

'Bring it to the roof terrace,' he yelled.

* * *

I rushed back to the kitchen, and brought him a bowl of wild mushroom risotto, and a tall glass of cherry-blueberry l-a-s-s-i. The guard moistens his lips and lowers his nose. He smells the risotto. Italian, I say. Foreign food, Major. You are a good man, he says. But you must never enter the art rooms. Only officers. Honest mistake, I say. Why are you trembling? he asks. Is it any good? I ask him. You are the *ustad* of cooking, he says. Serious, Major? I ask. Tell me. What do you think about the *Two Nudes*? He stares at the bowl. Come on, I say. You must have seen the painting. He tunes Agha's radio to the sports channel. India is playing West Indies in Barbados. The reception is crystal clear. Then I pour him rum.

'What do you think about the horses, Major?' I ask.

Horses, he says. The painter knows nothing about horses. How could one forget to show the most important thing, the horsehair . . . You are a good man, he says, but I don't want you to feed anyone else in this building. Is there a guest? I ask. There is the woman, he says, spooning the risotto. She's in the room next to the paintings, Major. She is a dangerous suicide bomber, he says. What is she doing here? Why is she not in a regular prison? I ask. He nods. I do not know. Perhaps she is here because this is the least likely place to find her, this is the cleverest way to dupe the enemy. She is still being interrogated. Officers come now and then to interrogate her.

Next day I visit the Guest House again. With new dishes. Duck vindaloo and cardamomed mango. The guard and I have lunch upstairs on the terrace. Major, I would like to interrogate her, I say. He laughs. His breath stinks of rum. And what are you going to ask her? Hazaar things, I say. Like what kind of food the enemy eats, what kind of dishes the enemy's General eats. How does he eat? How many times a day? Is he prone to diarrhea? Constipation? Does he fart? I will ask her very important questions. Plus I have Governor Sahib's orders to interrogate her.

'You have what?' he asks.

'Gen Sahib's permission and order to ask her the questions.'

'Major, in that case, I will open the room for you.'

But, that was not the real reason he unlocked the door.

'Here,' I said. 'Try some gulab jamun.'

25

The room had the worn look of colonial times. The carpet was dark and moldy and the bathroom door open. Close to the ceiling there were huge military bootprints stamped on the wall.

She was talking to herself. In Kashmiri.

When she felt my presence her body stirred a little. She did not raise her bent head. Her hair had grown back and it was wild and she did not have on the headscarf. I sat in the chair across from the bed. Her gaze remained fixed on the floor. There was a table in front of my chair. I opened my bag and pulled out two glasses and plates and spoons, and Coke and fish and biryani and placed everything on the table. Now and then sounds of guards marching outside penetrated the room, and sounds of dogs barking. The muezzin's call from a distant mosque penetrated as well.

I served her.

Not a single word had been exchanged between us so far. She ate slowly the fish and biryani, and I adopted her speed. Now and then I looked at her but our silence made the *looking* harder. I fixed my gaze on the bottle of Coke on the table. Bubbles at the top were bigger than the ones at the bottom. I wanted to ask her many questions. Instead, I was at a loss for words.

I heard her finish, and looked up. She was staring at me. The steel plate, still in her hand, was shining in the light.

'More biryani?' I asked.

She kept staring at me.

'I know you,' she said.

My hair was short now, no beard, and I had removed my turban. But she had recognized me.

'Why did you?' she asked.

'Because — '

The dogs were barking louder outside.

'I'll tell you later,' I said.

To prove to her my identity I had walked into the room with Chef's journal in the bag. But she had recognized me and there was no need to provide more proofs. That is why it was inappropriate to show her an *object* she could not even read.

'Do you recognize this?' I handed her the journal.

She seemed indifferent.

Then I said something I shouldn't have.

'He is dead,' I said.

'Who?'

'The man who wrote these pages.'

'Why are you telling me this?'

I moved to the edge of her bed.

'Why did you cut your hair?'

'Irem, you are for me — '

'Why did you?'

The next ten or fifteen minutes I told her everything about Kishen. Everything. I don't know why. Things I found difficult sharing with men in the barracks, I revealed to her in one single breath. At first she paid little attention to what I was saying, lost in some other world. Is she afraid? I asked myself. But somewhere down the line she grew drawn to Chef's address to the soldiers on the glacier.

'The biryani you consumed was really out of Chef's recipes,' I said.

'Same to same man who taught you Rogan Josh?'

I liked the way she said *same to same*.

'Same-to-same man whose journal you *read*,' I joked.

She was quiet again.

'No tomatoes in Rogan Josh,' I said.

Then I opened the journal. I didn't read everything. I censored many passages. But there were words even I had no control over. Forgiveness is a strange animal: I felt the need to ask her forgiveness. Otherwise I could not sit next to her. Could she forgive me for being from the *enemy* side? I read the journal to her: *Like most Indians I grew up prejudiced against Muslims. But unlike most of my country men I do not believe in caste. My difficult posting on the Siachen Glacier has taught me how tiny and fragile the human body is. It is a waste of time to be prejudiced. A waste of breath.*

She walked to the window. There was no window. She pretended there was a window. She stood there as if she was looking at the view outside. I knew what was outside: my cycle leaning against the plane tree, and next to it was the nurse's cycle. The nurse and I had failed to connect, but our cycles had met and they were making love to each other.

Thinking about the cycles I surveyed Irem's back, her long hair and its entanglements. She was facing the so-called window. We were six meters apart. Light was dim, same naked forty-watt bulb hanging from a naked wire. From where I sat, she looked healthy and plump. I stared at her hair and feet and back, her entire form. To amuse her, I think, yes, it was to amuse her, or perhaps to ease the tension I said she had grown *fat*, and suddenly her breathing grew heavy, and although I could only see her back I felt she was trying to grasp on to something, but there was nothing around her. She tried again, and again she failed. Then she turned.

277

She pivoted, suddenly uncomfortable, trying to protect herself from my gaze. The color of her face changed, and then parts of her body convulsed with bleak laughter, as if she was laughing at me. It was only then I realized she was heavy with a child.

'God,' I said.

I was at a loss for words.

'So . . . you are . . . you are not infertile!'

I did not know what else to say.

'Who?' I almost whispered. 'Who did it?'

She did not respond. She was not going to respond. It definitely could not be her husband in Pakistan. Who? Who was I going to report it to?

I was standing not far from the General's portrait on the wall, and all of a sudden I thought about the nurse's cycle propped against the plane tree outside. She was in the Raj Bhavan to give medication to little Rubiya. I thought of persuading the nurse to help Irem.

'The nurse,' I said.

'What about her?'

'She will take care of you?'

'How?'

'She will make your body normal again.'

'I do not want to be normal.'

'Please listen to me.'

'I am.'

'I want to help you. But I will only do so if you agree.'

'No,' she said.

'Would you like saffron?'

'Saffron?'

'Saffron, I have been told, causes miscarriage, and it works quickly, not causing much pain.'

'Please go away.'

'Think about it,' I said. 'Please.'

'Why are you humiliating me?'

'Humiliating you?'

'By asking again and again the same-to-same question.'

'You do not know what is good for you,' I said.

'Thank you for the biryani,' she said.

'Tomorrow. I will come again. Same time. I will knock on the door, and I will ask the same question. If you say yes, the nurse will help you.'

Then I picked up the empty plates and glasses from the table and stepped out. I felt very disturbed. I remember focusing on her back as I was stepping out. She was looking out of the so-called window. I almost turned, but restrained myself. I stood outside her door for a long time as if I wanted to listen to the sound of the 1.5 hearts beating inside her. I did not know what to do. To tell someone?

To tell someone and put her at more risk, and to put myself at risk?

Next day at the same time I knocked on the door and asked her the same-to-same question. But. She said no. I urged her to change her mind. The nurse would do it without telling anyone. The nurse will make you normal again. But she said no. She wanted to keep the child. She told me something women normally tell only their husbands. She told me the baby was kicking inside her belly. The baby was crying and asking her to give her a name. Don't be so emotional, I said. I have already given her a name, she said. What name? I asked.

Two days later I returned to the room again and begged her to allow me to take her home across the border. She said she did not want to return home. Her family was not going to accept her now. I am damaged, she said. Khuda is punishing me, she said, for my sins. Why did I not die? I should have died. It would have solved all troubles. I am not going to commit any more sins. I am going to keep the child.

There was a long silence. I walked to her and seized her hand. She was sitting on the edge of the bed. Again I urged her to allow me to take her to Pakistan. But the moment I uttered the word 'Pakistan' she fell back on the bed. Her whole body convulsed, and her two hands started opening the drawstring of her salwar, and there she was partially unconscious and partially unclothed on the bed, with the naked bulb above us. It was at that point the ayah entered the room. I do not know from where she came and why, but she saw. She saw us together. Then walked in the guard, and then marched in the colonel in his trussed jacket.

Four

26

From the bus I saw the General's private car. The driver was holding my name written in huge letters. I *am* cancer, and I have arrived in Kashmir. I sat in the front seat and the driver checked with me if I was comfortable there, and I nodded, and asked him to drive slowly. His face looked vaguely familiar. The sun was setting. There were plane trees on both sides of the road. The car sped up as it looped around the army camp on the slopes of the mountain. I turned in my seat and tried to locate the spot where the army had put up the tents to court-martial me.

Schoolchildren were playing there, at the exact same spot. They did not know a thing. Neither about me, nor about the court martial. Troops were marching outside the camp. *One-two-three. One-two-three.* I must have been lost in deep thought because I didn't notice when the car started winding up the hill to the Raj Bhavan. There was a deep mist in the mountains, not much was visible. I must have looked towards the Mughal garden with longing, and perhaps that is why the driver turned to me and said, 'Stop first at the garden, sir?'

'Yes, yes,' I said, surveying the ruins.

But then I changed my mind, and asked him to hurry to the Governor's residence. On the way I noticed lots of checkposts and military bunkers and (to my surprise) beauty parlors. Dal Lake had more weeds now, and the signs by the road said that the weeds were being removed by a Swiss company. The golf course, on my right, was deserted. The chenar trees looked ancient, bare, ready to receive snow.

The car passed between the two gateposts and guards, and stopped in front of the Raj Bhavan. The flag of our country was fluttering on the post. The servant who was standing by the entrance saluted me and rushed to the car to pick up my trunk and bag. I told him not to, but he picked up the two items anyway, and dashed indoors. A hospital jeep was parked by the fence. I hit a stone on the way to the house, and stumbled for a while.

'Where are you going, sir?' asked a voice. I was heading towards the rear entrance, but the voice made me yield to it. He was the General's new ADC. Suddenly it occurred to me how much time had passed, and for no reason I touched the stone pillar at the front.

The ADC asked me to wait in the living room. The room looked both strange and familiar with its carpets, fireplace, rashtrapati furniture, and glass cabinets. I occupied the walnut chair in the corner, and looked out the window.

'Who is that lady with a little dog and a cell phone?' I asked.

She was standing on the terrace of the Guest House.

'Her name is Mrs Ramani, sir. She is the previous Governor's daughter.'

'Yes, yes, I know.'

Her peace paisley silk was fluttering in the wind. She had climbed up the stairs of the Guest House for a clear cell phone reception, and was yakking away. So this is Bina after fourteen years, I said to myself. Still beautiful but no longer the same one whose wedding banquet I took care of.

'What is she doing here?' I asked.

'Bedding guest, sir.'

'Bedding guest?'

'No, sir. Bedding guest.'

'Wedding guest?'

'Yessir.' Sitting in the walnut chair I felt very tired. I felt like my journey had come to an end and yet had come to nothing. I felt like returning to Delhi.

'Ready-made tea, sir?'

'Sorry?' I asked.

His fingers were grubby. He was the new Chef's assistant.

'Ready-made chai, sir?'

'No milk and sugar in my tea.'

'Sir.'

'Wait,' I said.

'Sir.'

'What is that white slab in the lawn?'

'The dog, sir.'

'When did it happen?'

'Don't know, sir.'

He left tea and Marie biscuits on the table in front of my chair. The tea was horrible, no cardamom and excess ginger.

Sipping tea I asked myself if my need to cling to life was so enormous that I had forgotten my morals. I thought of all the people who will attend the wedding banquet dressed in peace silk and paisley, and they will talk as if all was well and all will be well. They will eat tandoori chicken and mint chutney and mango pudding and drink Bailey's chai. And the things they will say about Rubiya's choice of a husband. They would have said things anyway, they always do, but this time they will say more as if they were entitled, and the few who will fly in from Pakistan will display their suave French-cuff shirts, and they will wine and dine and dance and repeat the same worn-out phrases — 'Give us your Bombay actress Madhuri' and 'Take our Kashmir!' and no one will pay any attention to people like Irem. People like her do not matter. Damaged people like her do not matter at all. Even when they leave the hospitals they remain sick. Even when they leave prisons they remain trapped. Their sickness is being alive. Their crime is that they continue to exist.

The wedding guests will say, The curry did not have right enough masala. While others after a few bottles will say, Curry karari thee, bahout khoob sahib, bahut khoob. Gazab ka korma. Subhan Allah, the Hindus will say. Some will speak English with English accents and some will display polished American accents and say, The curry was not done yet, or some other infantile thing, like the curry was fun-tastic, very good hanh. Someone else in broken English will say, Ever since my wife die-vorced me I have not had this kind of curry, and then someone will correct the man, It is 'divorce' not 'die-vorce'. Yes, yes, that is what I meant, the other would say. Why am I here? What am I doing here? I asked myself in the walnut chair.

Soon the ADC led me to the General's room. The corridor was unusually cold. He walked fast, and I walked slow, but finally both of us stood in front of the door. The curtains were swaying.

It must have been a slight hesitation on my

side that made the ADC literally push me inside. General Sahib was standing in front of the window, hands crossed behind his back, one hand trembling.

On the little circular table not far from his bed a cigarette — half-consumed and hurriedly extinguished — released a few threads of smoke.

Not knowing what to do, I clicked my heels. The General turned and said, 'Jai Hind' and walked towards me and shook hands and then he almost hugged me, but something made him change his mind. His hand started trembling violently.

'Kirpal, how is your mother?'

'Not well, sir.'

He sat at the edge of his bed and pointed towards the armchair.

'Please sit down.'

This was the first time I had received such an honor, and perhaps that is why I hesitated again.

'Sit down,' he said, 'Sorry there is smoke in the room. I have just seen the doctor. After the doctor leaves I always have to smoke.'

'No problem, sir.'

'We knew.'

'Sir.'

'You would come. You would not fail us.'

'Sir.'

'Rubiya will be pleased,' he said. 'You came because of her?'

I sensed that the General wanted to have a long conversation, but his breath was coming out with a wheeze.

'Take your bath. Drink water. Rest. Don't forget you are in the mountains now. We will have dinner together.'

He rang the bell.

The servant appeared.

'Keep the bags in the Guest House.'

'Sir,' I said, 'if you don't mind I am staying in a hotel.'

'Your room is ready.'

'Please, sir. If you do not mind.'

'In that case, Kirpal, my car will take you there.'

'Thank you, sir.'

'We must have a quick word.'

'Sir.'

'Rum?' asked the General.

'No, thank you, sir.'

On the way to the Raj Bhavan I had thought of the possibility of facing him alone, and I knew he was waiting for it and I tried to predict his questions. I, too, had questions. So much time had passed and the questions had acquired a huge weight. Looking at the frail form of General Sahib now I felt like delaying them. Things had to sort out between us, but not right away. Looking at the plane trees outside the window, bare tops swaying in the wind, I felt like experiencing one last bright moment of Kashmir, it was enough for that day of my arrival. 'After you left did your cooking change?' he asked.

'Very right, sir. I have discovered that simplicity is the main principle of cooking. My dishes are growing simpler and simpler.'

'So I will begin with a simple question,' he said. 'Why did you leave, Kirpal?'

He looked through me and I was unable to say a word.

'For all official purposes it was the health of your mother, Kirpal. The court martial cleared your name. The army sent an official apology and compensation afterwards. The circumstantial evidence said that you were guilty. But that enemy woman said you were not guilty.'

'Her name is Irem, sir.'

'Yes, yes — I know. She had not even filed charges against you. So why did you leave?'

I was not able to say a word.

'I think I know why you left,' he said. 'All these years I have tried to answer this question, but I want to ask you if there is an iota of truth in this. You were like my son, Kirpal, and your father was well-like. He was my finest officer. I know why you left. I know it. You fell in love with her. You were in love with that woman. That is why you left.'

He looked at me again in the eye.

'You loved her the way Rubiya loves this man from Pakistan. I had told Rubiya no matter what happens the boy will not step inside this house. What right does Rubiya have to act on her desires the way she did? Tell me. When you were completely in love with that enemy woman, when you could control your desires, then why not Rubiya?'

Because I was at a loss for words the General continued.

'Sometimes I think the desire for the enemy is more than the desire for our own. No one knows this better than you. And that is why you left. That was the real reason. You did not want to act on your desire. You did not want to. You saw a villain or two. And that was the easy way out. You saw the villain and left. And you did not even have the courage to tell me the truth. But how could you have told me? I was the one more powerful. I was like your father, Kirpal. But you used your *ailing* mother to deal with something you could not deal with. Your mother's sickness became the veil to hide behind. And because you did not talk about the problem you thought the problem did not exist. Now say something.'

'Sir.'

His breathing grew heavier.

'I wanted Rubiya to be here. In a way it is good she is not here. God knows where she is. After all I have done to you, will you, still be kind enough to be the chef at her wedding? Civil wedding. It is going to be a small affair. Twenty, thirty people. The boy's family is coming by bus from the Pakistani-occupied Kashmir.'

'Of course, sir.'

'Everything must be perfect. This is Rubiya's wedding. Everything must be ek-dum perfect.'

'Sir, you have my word. But.'

'I knew there was a BUT.'

'No, sir. I would just like to have a word with Ms Rubiya. Regarding the menu, sir.'

27

The general's private car has just dropped me at Hotel Liward. My legs are stiff and my whole body is aching. I am thinking about the long bus journey after the long train journey. Every part of the bus rattled for eleven hours on the mountain road. Every window. Now every bone in my body is protesting. The bus to Srinagar took eleven hours, and for eleven hours my body had to suffer. Perhaps I should say my body behaved unusually well on the way. A man, much younger than me, vomited six or seven times, but my body cooperated, and I threw up only two or three times, or perhaps this is just a lie. It is impossible to lie to oneself. Just like it is impossible to tickle oneself. Only mad people tickle themselves. I am not mad. I made a big mistake to set out on this tedious journey.

It is for Rubiya's sake really I am here. Otherwise I would not have come to the valley. Yet. It is for my own sake really I am here. I know once I do the perfect banquet, General Sahib will refer me to top specialists in the military hospital, and they will start treatment right away.

On the road to Srinagar, a sign said:

This is neither a race, nor a rally.
Drive safely in Kashmir valley.

These people are real jokers. I hear the bleak laughter of Kashmiris everywhere. Even in the hotel room.

My room is big and it has a large hot brazier and a mirror on the wall. The bed is neatly made; there is an extra quilt in the closet. I complained (about the small room 'S' they had allotted me earlier) and the manager moved me to this VIP room: 'N'. (The rooms are not numbered. I wonder why they are lettered?) Climbing up the stairs made me breathless. I unlocked 'N' and took off my cap and overcoat. On the wall two hairline cracks and the oval mirror. Looking inside, a sudden memory returned to me of that day when Father had helped me untie my shoes after a long journey. I was four or five years old then. My eyes fluttered, reliving the memory. I felt a lump in my throat as I undressed. Then I stepped into the bathroom and washed my hands and face.

★ ★ ★

I am unable to sleep. I walk to the window. I open it and shut it properly. Chilly outside. I see a Sufi shrine and a post office. The light is dim. The post office is closed. I want to say something. The word does not come to my mouth. What was it I would like to say? What exactly is wrong with my brain? The b-u-s. I wonder why I spoke to the woman in the bus?

We were sitting next to each other. Me: on the window seat. In the beginning we did not exchange a word, but the driver's rash turns on the winding road made her say something and I nodded and then we could not stop talking. For five and a half hours, almost half of the way, we were silent to each other, lost in our own worlds, and then suddenly we started talking, and I overexerted myself. There was no need to do it. I even offered her my window seat, but she said the aisle was better.

She was a Kashmiri Hindu woman, returning home after a gap of thirteen years. She said her situation was a bit like the exiles in the epic Mahabharata. I apologized for my limited knowledge of Hindu epics. I grew up in the Sikh tradition, I confessed. She studied my face carefully. So why, *sardar-ji*, have you cut your hair and removed your turban?

I said nothing.

My husband had a travel agency in

Srinagar, she told me, and I used to teach biology in school, classes 6, 7 and 8; but we were forced out of the city by the militants. Deep down all Muslims are pro-Pakistan, she said. Our servant was an exception, she said. He would send us letters about the house, now the house is with the militants, he would write, and now it is with the army or paramilitary, but in the last letter he told us that the house was empty, and the roof of what used to be the kitchen and the bedroom had fallen in.

Listening to her I thought of those moments lost to time, my first arrival in Kashmir when Chef took me on long bike rides, plane leaves rustling under the tires, ruins on left, and ruins on right, and so many empty houses, and once or twice he had said that the city without the Kashmiri Hindus looked incomplete. Why, Chef?

'Without the Hindus (who have been forced to flee by some Muslim extremists) this valley looks exactly like *Swiss cheese*,' he said.

'*Cheeze?*'

His comment initially left me confused. *Cheeze* means a 'thing' in my mother tongue. Punjabi, the only language in the world made entirely out of puns . . .

I am talking about paneer, Kirpal. *Swiss*

cheese is a strange variety of paneer with holes in it. In school they taught us: *Kashmir India ka Switzerland hai.* Well, this place has certainly become the 'Swiss cheese of India'. When I look at the empty Hindu houses in the valley, Kirpal, I realize there is no bigger tragedy for a land that forces its own people out and makes them wander from place to place, and leaves them damaged with an intense longing to return home.

The woman changed her seat. She found one next to a peasant girl just before the bus entered the three-mile-long tunnel. Whenever a woman sitting next to me changes seats I ask myself if I did something wrong. She had a plastic bag full of cherry tomatoes, and she kept eating them one by one. She did not offer me a single tomato. Did I misbehave? Did I offend her with a swear word? Do I have bad breath? Did I utter something very lucid? Islands of lucidity are forming inside my brain. Did I mutter something on love? I have wasted the years of my life being too much in love. Love that was not even returned. Love for the wrong person or a thing. Love is a dish that is either overcooked or undercooked. Love never tastes right. Love smells like the inside of a garbage bag. Love has the odor of decay. Throw it away.

I unpack my suitcase. Breathless again.

There is a little package for Rubiya. And a gift for someone else. My clothes have all tangled up in each other. The jacket and pants and the tie I brought along from Delhi need ironing. They will look good on you, Mother had said. They will look good on you, Kip.

I don't deserve to wear these things. They are too bloody new.

I have the breath of death, I say to myself in the hotel room. Women sense it more than men. And they do not want to get closer. In a way I felt relieved when the woman moved because I was able to stretch, but an old man occupied the empty seat minutes after she vacated it. She never once looked back and kept eating her tomatoes. She did not notice her replacement. He was a Muslim man, conical cap on head. Hooked nose. He was using a toothpick to clean his teeth. As he settled on the seat, the man asked, What time is it, jenab? I noticed he had a watch on his wrist, and I assumed it must have broken and I told him the time, and he thanked me — shoorkriya jenab, he said — but right after the tunnel in bright light I noticed the man's watch was showing the correct time.

Inside the Jawahar tunnel we had to shut the bus windows. The driver feared a militant grenade or an improvised explosive. Inside

300

the tunnel water kept dripping from rock. The tunnel is three miles long. For three long miles yellow sodium lamps lit the road. Then the light of Kashmir appeared. Blue mountains. Bright numinous light reached out to touch us. The driver, that idiot, put the bus in neutral and coasted all the way downhill. Coasting saves him diesel. Just before hitting the valley he asked us, the passengers, to look towards the right. Verinag, he said. This is where the river begins, he said. As if we did not know.

The bus was coasting down. The tunnel disappeared behind us in the crack of the mountain. A few miles later it reappeared. I looked upwards from the window seat and noticed the arch of the tunnel. The happiness and unhappiness of so many people depends on the tunnel and the road, and the road to Kashmir is not so bad. The buses are, the drivers are, the checkposts are. If there is one thing right about our country it is the road.

From my hotel window I can see the Hindu houses. They have been empty for so long, the roofs are falling in. It has been ages since someone burned fire in those rooms. No smoke rises out of chimneys. Time is mocking the chimneys. In one of those kitchens I would like to cook for both Hindus and Muslims.

The difference between Hindu cuisine and Muslim cuisine is very easy to explain. In Kashmir the Hindus avoid sexy onions and garlic; they love the taste of heeng (asafetida) and the non-incestuous fennel and ginger. Muslims find heeng (and its sulphurous odor) unbearable. They adore garlic, green praans, garam masala, and on certain occasions, mawal flowers. So there is a 'Hindu' Rogan Josh, and a 'Muslim' Rogan Josh. Over the years I have developed my own recipe, a Rogan Josh inspired by these two great traditions. I have perfected the dish, and I can say without hesitation that it is my finest accomplishment. Rogan Josh is red because of Kashmiri chilies, which are ten times more red than the ordinary Indian mirchis. I know this from Irem. I must discuss the menu yet with Rubiya, but I will manage to persuade her to allow me to prepare this delicacy at the wedding.

Rogan Josh
900g lamb (shoulder cut, with or without bones), well rinsed and sliced into one-inch rectangles
5 tablespoons ghee
1 cup dahi
6 cloves, crushed finely
2 tablespoons Kashmiri red chili powder

1 cinnamon stick
½ teaspoon turmeric powder
1 onion, finely chopped
1 tablespoon ginger-garlic paste
4–5 garlic cloves, minced or finely sliced
2 teaspoons ginger powder
2 teaspoons fennel powder
1 teaspoon cumin seeds
¼ teaspoon cumin powder
¼ teaspoon crushed cardamom
1 teaspoon garam masala
½ teaspoon heeng
14 strands of saffron

Marinate the lamb for two hours. Coat the pieces with ginger-garlic paste, cumin powder, crushed cardamom, and turmeric. Sprinkle salt (to taste).

Heat ghee on high flame in a large heavy-bottomed pot (for best results, use degchi).

Add cloves, cumin, heeng, and cinnamon. Sauté for 2 minutes.

Add onion. Sauté until golden.

Add garlic. Sauté for 2 minutes.

Add lamb. Sear until dark brown on all sides. Oily juice will come out of pieces.

Stir till all liquid in the pot becomes vapor. Make sure the meat pieces don't stick to the bottom.

Add dahi (well whisked) one spoon at a time, stirring constantly.

Cook for 15 minutes on medium heat.

Stir constantly till the sauce becomes very thick. Make sure the meat pieces don't stick to the bottom.

Now add Kashmiri red chili 'liquid' (chili powder dissolved in 2 cups of hot water). Stir well.

Switch to high heat.

Add ginger and fennel powder. Stir and bring the pot to boil.

Cover and cook on low heat till the lamb is tender (approximately an hour).

Now add garam masala.

Cook for 2 or 3 minutes more.

Now add 'liquid saffron' and stir well. To prepare the liquid: Crush the saffron threads and mix with two tablespoons of hot water.

Rogan Josh is done.

Serves 6

Rogan Josh is done, I say to myself on the bed in the hotel room. Dinner is ready, Sahib . . . Drinks are served, Sahib . . . Applause . . . Shabash . . . Applause . . . I recall with absolute clarity that Sunday, *five years ago*, when the army honored me for my culinary contributions at the Military Academy in

Dehradun. After the ceremony I delivered a small talk on Kashmiri cuisine for trainee chefs, jawans and officers and their wives, which was very well received, so many stood up and gave me genuine heartfelt applause. Standing ovation, as Sahib would have said.

During the little break (just before my talk) I wandered off towards the beautiful lawns of the Academy, and there under a tree I saw a cadet in uniform reading a book. I was filled with curiosity and inquired about the title, and he said it was a book of poems, and it was called *In Different Hours*. I flipped through the book, looked at the author's name, and found myself saying out loud: So our Rubiya has become a poet.

'You know the poet, sir?'

'Of course. She used to taste my food. Rubiya was the taster of my preparations. I am so happy she has become a poet.'

'I can't believe you know her, sir,' the cadet said again, somewhat stunned.

'Yes, yes, General Kumar's daughter has become a poet.'

'Sir.'

'Only yesterday she was playing with toys in the garden.'

'I would like to write to her, sir. Please would you be kind enough to introduce me to the poet?'

So I wrote a little note of introduction for the young man, and jotted down my own address on a sheet of paper. I do not know how he got hold of her address or if he received a response, but to my surprise I received a response from Rubiya. She sent me two new poems as well, and a cutting of the newspaper article she had written after a recent trip to Pakistan. When I read the article I knew that the fate of Kashmir was going to change. I said to myself that this was the right approach. Not what Chef Kishen did. Chef's approach was wrong. The path that Rubiya is following is the correct one, I had said to myself, and I say it again to myself, now, in this hotel room. When I read that article by Rubiya I knew that from now on the fate of Kashmir was going to change.

Before I flew to Pakistan, every day I had to deal with my fear of the border. The day I turned 5, Father drove us on a jeep to the border. It was a flag meeting, which is usually rare at that most unforgiving border. I was afraid, unable to articulate my fear. I found it difficult to cross the Line to Pakistan. 'If you cannot make up your mind,' said the guard on the Indian side, 'then run back to the jeep.' I still remember the paralysis I experienced standing in the gravitational

306

field of the Line. Now and then I am able to recall the distance between the line (on the ground) and my foot (right above the line) frozen in air. My father had already crossed to the other side, the wrong side, and I was engulfed with strange and familiar fears. 'Come, come,' beckoned the enemy guard with a smile. But I could not overcome the terror, which kept swelling inside me. I ran back to the jeep. From the jeep I saw my father talking to enemy uncles and aunties as if they were his half-cousins.

Rubiya wrote a monthly column in the paper. I started reading her articles regularly. She never once mentioned me in her writings. I was a little bit hurt. Especially by the original article she had sent me in the letter. She had completely omitted me. I had accompanied her and General Sahib on that trip to the border. I had comforted her, given her her favorite badam kheer to eat. Not her ayah. The ayah was sick that day. And I had taken care of Rubiya that day. Only after reading the article the third or the fourth time I stopped feeling hurt. I know she did not mention me because it was to protect me. I was, it is safe to say, very important in her upbringing. I think she knows this so well she does not want to embarrass me with outwardly praise.

Rubiya and I, a long time ago, had developed a special understanding, which goes beyond words. (Am I repeating myself?) Sometimes when General Sahib was a little annoyed with my performance, Rubiya would wink or give me a look, which meant, I understand, don't worry, my father is a bit out of his mind. He is a bit fussy, that is all.

I was not even seven when my mother died. At first things were difficult, she was absent and present everywhere I went, wounding me. Father was sad too and we would walk hours on end without talking to each other. Few months later he and I watched a movie at the open-air cinema in the army campus. Soon this became a ritual. He would accompany me to watch old Bollywood films. Seating at the cinema was strictly according to one's rank. The chairs close to the screen were earmarked for officers and their families. Non-commissioned officers and combat soldiers and orderlies and cooks and gardeners could watch only from behind the screen. They sat cross-legged on grass, facing the projectionist, in strange lotus postures. Men in hobnailed boots guarded the border between the two sides. Once the heroine on the screen nearly drowned in monsoon rain. This scene was so intense, it left the guards leaning on their rifles, and I walked to the other side.

There were more insects on the other side and they bit me hard, but what struck me the most was that the image on the screen looked utterly different. Some mysterious power, I felt, had transformed the symmetry on the screen. Our 'left' was their 'right', and our 'right' was their 'left'. Fundamentally, nothing changed; rain did not become saliva, the coin-sized mirrors on the heroine's sari did not turn to fire, and yet after that incident never have I been able to look at moving images without hearing sounds of soldiers marching, and never have I been able to walk without thinking about the symmetry or the break in symmetry.

Now, many years later, I think the border between India and Pakistan is a bit like the white film screen that belonged to the open-air cinema. Both sides happen to be watching the same film, sometimes projected from India and sometimes from the Pakistani side, and our left is their right, and our right is their left.

Her bold articles in the paper gave me courage, a lot of courage, and perhaps that is why I finally wrote to her about Irem. After that I did not hear from Rubiya for a long time. She skipped her weekly column in the paper, and this made me worry. But a huge piece appeared three weeks later focusing entirely on Irem. In the article she had changed Irem's name. She had called her Soofiya. She had found Irem in a prison.

I felt overjoyed and yet I felt very sad. Because I had written my note to Rubiya six years too late.

Rubiya's article on Irem was very long. But there are fragments which keep coming back to me over and over again. She wrote:

Soofiya found that she was pregnant. She was offered an abortion, which she refused. She gave birth to a baby girl she named Naseem, which means the morning breeze.

Soofiya served out her sentence for 'entering India illegally' but no one told her that now she was free to go. The story got out because of an ex-army man's anonymous letter to an Indian NGO. The letter was forwarded to the World Human Rights Protection Council. Because of the intervention, the Indian authorities sent Soofiya and Naseem on a police-escorted vehicle to the Line of Control. But the Pakistani border guards refused entry. 'We will allow Soofiya in,' said the guards. 'But we will not allow the girl — she, like her 'father', is really an Indian citizen.'

Four more attempts were made. With similar results. In the meantime Naseem has started the prison school in Indian Kashmir. She is a bright kid brimming with curiosity. Soofiya fully approves of her daughter's education; at times she brags before the prison immates about Naseem's ability to read and write. The last few days all I have thought about is this . . . That time is running out . . . The rough muscular talk between the Hindu fundamentalist leaders of my country, India, and the Pakistani dictator, General Musharraf, has escalated beyond comprehension. Both sides are promising a 'total' war. In 1998 when the two countries had tested nuclear weapons in the desert sands the same leaders had promised that atomic weapons were really a deterrence . . . Last week the two armies marched to the border again, a million men in combat-ready positions. Anti-personnel and anti-tank mines have been planted all along the 1800-mile border. The air smells of the end of the world . . . During times like these it seems foolhardy to focus on an ordinary woman and her daughter.

And yet. I feel the story of Soofiya and little Naseem is the story of the whole of Kashmir.

28

What hurts a person into poetry? I ask myself. What made Rubiya a poet? The plane leaves? Snow, or night, or the death of her mother? Or the food she ate? What are the things one must do for the sake of a single poem? Where does poetry come from? As a child she was always hiding from grown-ups. She would make herself small, hiding under the bed or the table, hiding from her father. She sat under a dark table reading books. She played with the black dog. She tried to catch butterflies in the lawn, separating herself from the rest. She refused my meals. The ayah would not allow her to enter the kitchen. Was she becoming a poet then? Did she write he first poem when she first heard about the glacier?

Where are you headed, Papa?
To the glacier.
Who lives there?
Our men, the soldiers.
It is funny, Papa. It must be so easy to slide down.

When exactly does one become a poet?
But, Dad?
Yes, Rubiya.
*If the glacier is moving, then how do the
two armies draw the line?*
What do you mean?
*How do India and Pakistan tell where
the border is precisely?*

When exactly?

Just before her wedding, when I would
meet her alone I would ask her all these
questions. I would tell her: Rubiya, your
poems have made me happy. You will make so
many people happy. Millions in our country,
and also in the 'enemy' country, will be
comforted by these words.

'Are you going to write a poem about your
father?' I would ask her.

'Chef Kirpal,' she would respond, 'poetry
is not cooking. Poets do not get to choose.
It is the poem that chooses the poet.'

Afterwards

Then you will go to Kashmir
in no hurry
and hear not a single fire

The blessed women
will paint
saffron on your skin
and you will build a house there,
and weave a basket for pomegranates,
and glaze pots in fire
The jagged mountains
will no longer weep
slow muddy tears
or tremble behind
dwarf trees anymore.

Sit. There on encrusted ice
— they will ask you —
Look how it gleams, feel it moving.
Dust the nozzles
of fountains in Shalimar Bagh
in the ruined Nishat Bagh
— they will ask you —
Plant paisley
in one or two cemeteries
where shade bites
the sun. The women

will lead you to damp green
shrines of Noor-u-din. There
you will locate one or two eggs in nests
and mounds of cricket balls
and lost men, too, and
schoolchildren.

Bright smiles
will mark them from the rest, just like
the tattoo on your skin
marked you. In autumn —
you will write long letters
addressed to your old self —
a profusion of dots and dashes . . .
Old photographs, defeats, loves, recipes
you will move the entire attic
to an unfinished room
and hire
a strong houseboat and help.

Yes, your old forgotten self —
the stranger will paddle you
to the shadows of never
pruned
plane trees. There — in autumn in
Kashmir

the two of you would meet. By the roots
and barks and
Technicolor leaves
and millions of dead.
Don't just sit there. Smell them.

On the second day of my arrival — the eighth
of December — when I woke up in the hotel
room I read in the paper that just after eleven
o'clock the previous night General Kumar

had killed himself. He had eaten dinner with Rubiya, and after saying goodnight to her he returned to his room. The servant served tea, and the General took his medication; half an hour later he shot himself. He used the defeated Pakistani general's pistol from the glass cabinet, and fired only once through his left jaw to do the job.

The paper made no mention of Rubiya's wedding plans or the postponement of the wedding. The front-page editorial talked about his sickness, the battle with disease, and praised the Hero of Kargil and the Hero of Siachen Glacier for exceptional leadership and vision.

He took over the Governorship of Kashmir, the editorial said, when the State was going through a particularly difficult time.

General Sahib was cremated on the slopes of the hill overlooking the river, not far from the ruins of the Mughal fort. Thin layers of ice on the banks of the river turned orange, reflecting the flames. A three-minute silence was observed before Rubiya offered her father's body to nothingness. The battles stopped on distant mountains and transistor radios stopped and vehicles stopped on the roads and cooking and eating stopped. People paused, interrupted whatever they were doing.

During those three minutes I heard restrained sobbing coming from the Kashmiri houses. Then agni, the burst of flames. The shadow of rising smoke flickered on the hard ground. The December chill disappeared temporarily. A can of Coke fell from an old woman's hand and rolled towards the black boots of troops in ceremonial dress.

The military band was part of the ceremony. Men in kilts played mournful bagpipes and snared the drums. Troops from *1 Sikh* gave a twenty-one gun salute. Two or three dogs kept running by the ice, absolutely oblivious of the flag of our country, flying at half-mast. And all those who stood there, the officers and jawans and their wives, they had no idea about the battles the General was really fighting. They spoke in clichés, and they stared accusingly at Rubiya as if she had caused her father's death. There are decent boys in our own country, their faces said, Why don't you marry one of our own? Colonel Chowdhry and Patsy Chowdhry were absent, but so many others were there. Bina was there, holding a paisley hanky, weeping profusely. For nothing.

'General Sahib, *good man dee lal-tain*,' I raised my voice. 'General Sahib, Emperor of Kulfi.'

'What are you saying, sir?' asked the young

officer standing next to me.

'Nothing. Gibberish. Bakwas.'

★ ★ ★

Three days later I met Rubiya in the Mughal garden. I had arranged to meet her at three in the afternoon, but I got delayed.

She was looking at the children playing in snow as I walked in. The children had on two or three layers of heavy woolens and they were making balls of ice. There was snow on the ground, on trees, on ruined walls and fountains. Everything sparkled.

At first I saw only her back. Then I climbed up the stairs and saw her from the pavilion. She was looking at the children as if she wanted to tell them that the world was not what they had thought it was. I did not feel like disturbing her.

When she turned towards me the first thing she said was, 'Chef Kirpal, you smell of rum.'

She looked younger than her age, and very sad.

She told me that her fiancé, Shahid, and his parents had been denied visas at the border, so she was heading to Pakistan on the evening bus.

But I am really here to tell you about Irem, Chef Kirpal. Irem and her daughter are back in Pakistan now. After many years the Pakistani authorities have allowed them to return home.

I don't know why at that time I did not tell her about my cancer. Or the fact that my feet were very cold.

Instead I found myself talking about a cooking show on television, but as soon as I did that I was worried for her, and I wanted to urge her to stay. I worried Rubiya would not be safe in Pakistan, just like Irem was not safe in India.

'Before you go,' I asked her, 'is it possible to apologize for my behavior?'

'Why?'

'Because I waited for very long to write to you about Irem.'

'You have done nothing wrong,' she said. 'You are the nicest person I have come across.'

'No, I am not nice,' I said.

'Please, what are you trying to say?'

'Something has been bothering me, Rubiya. This thing happened on the way. I took the bus. The driver was very rash on the winding road. You know the way they drive. He was off the road most of the time and almost ran into an army convoy. Soon afterwards the bus collided with a pack of sheep, badly wounding an animal. The animal was squirming in great pain. It was dying. The gujjar shepherds yelled at the driver from the road, and began knocking. But all the passengers inside wanted the driver to hurry up. No one cared about the animal. I, too, wanted the bus-wallah to hurry. We all had something *important* to get to, and there we were aimed in a great rush, and no one thought of slowing down. No, Rubiya. I am not very nice. I am more like my countrymen. That makes me more, not less, ashamed of them.'

'Chef Kirpal,' she said, 'I sense you have some other thing to tell me.'

'There is one question that has been growing inside me for the last fourteen years. May I ask?'

She nodded.

'It is a question that has acquired the weight of a glacier,' I said. 'And I don't say it lightly. When I try to ask the question, I feel paralyzed. Words freeze in my mouth. Rubiya, do you understand me?'

She wanted me to continue.

'Please, this is really a question for Irem. But I must ask you because you know a lot of things about her. If Irem were walking here with us today, I would have asked her the same question.'

Irem was pregnant, I said. There were visible signs. It took me a while to open my eyes, but the signs were there. I saw them. She was pregnant. The court martial took place in the Badami Bagh camp. She told the presiding officer that I was not guilty. She had not even charged me. The legal officer had charged me. She withdrew the false charges. The court martial presiding officer cleared me. But the question remained. Someone did that thing. Who? Why? The press published the story that in a way closed the case. The papers reported that the 'prison guard' would enter her room every night and take advantage of her. The 'prison guard' was a Muslim, the papers said. Irem received a letter from him after the court martial, the papers said. 'If she promises not to take me to the court, I am willing to marry her,' the guard had written. I wanted to believe this. But I could not. If she knew it was the guard who did it, then why did she not charge him earlier, during my court martial? She knew that I did not do it, and when the court saw me as guilty she withdrew all the charges. But she refrained from naming the real culprit. To be honest, when I pleaded not guilty, I suspected the General himself, and a few other officers, were guilty. But I did not say a word. I was not sure.

★ ★ ★

Rubiya and I were walking in the garden when it started to snow. Dry symmetrical crystals started falling on her black coat. Slowly, then fast. The children were far away from us, happy, playing in the snow. At first we did not seem to mind. But soon took shelter in a tea stall by the gates of the garden.

'Two cups,' I ordered.

'I am paying,' she said.

'No, I am older. I am paying.'

Smoke of hookah mixed with bakerkhani, the Kashmiri pastry, inside the tea stall. Smell of freshly baked bread filled the air. Not far from us two old men were breaking the bread, and sipping kehva tea. Outside, snow was falling slowly on military vehicles. On tombstones. On Sufi shrines. On ruined wooden houses. Big flakes, tens and thousands, swirled in the air. Tens and thousands settled on grass no longer green. Flakes were accumulating on Kashmir the way people in Delhi accumulate on trains. She took off her long coat. Shook her hair. Snow fell down.

I continued: In the beginning I only suspected, but then something happened that made me absolutely sure. That day, a few weeks after the court martial, when the house was being rearranged Irem had shown up with a green bag. I do not know how she got out of the prison or how she entered the Raj Bhavan complex. Pretending to be a worker in the kitchen perhaps. Taking advantage of the lax security. Security is not always tight. I saw her enter. I saw everything from the kitchen window. There were vegetables in the bag and she dug her hand in the bag and pulled out a vegetable, then put it back in the bag. She repeated this kind of movement several times as if unable to make up her mind. I saw everything through the window. She had chosen the precise moment when most soldiers step down the hill to the barracks for lunch. And she was going to throw a *vegetable* in the General's room. General Sahib was inside, resting, and you Rubiya were outside, playing. She knew this. The thing in her hand looked like a vegetable, but it was not a vegetable, as I discovered later. It was a grenade. Made in Pakistan. But she did not throw the grenade. She changed her mind. I saw her struggle. Her hand touched her heart and she turned and then turned back as if she was looking at the house for one last time and disappeared behind the plane trees. I ran out of the kitchen after she had long disappeared. She had *forgotten* the bag by the verandah and I brought the bag into the kitchen and one by one I placed the things on the table and it was then I found the grenade. It was clear: she had meant to kill the General, and I understood why, but I never understood one thing. Why did she change her mind? Was it because she saw you, Rubiya, playing nearby? And she could not imagine making that child an orphan?

Rubiya did not say anything.

I threw the grenade into the river. I never reported the incident. Then resigned from the army. Rubiya, do you know where the bag is? I threw it away with the vegetables in the river. And the moment I threw it away I knew what to do next.

Rubiya's elbows were on the table and her head between her hands.

'Chef Kirpal,' she said.

I remained quiet because I knew now she would tell me something on her own. There was water from melted snow on her brow and I felt like wiping it but I knew it might interrupt what she was about to say, so I did nothing. Her long jacket, dangling from the peg on the wall, had snow on it, as did the tips of her shoes. I had wiped my shoes clean, but my glasses were covered with little melted drops.

The tea-wallah was yelling at his assistant.

'Sahib, Memsahib, kehva!' The owner brought us the cups himself. There were strands of saffron floating on top.

'For special cases,' the owner told us, 'I have a room upstairs. No one will dis-ta-rub you up there.'

How mistaken that man was about the nature of our relationship. But we decided to move anyway.

The stairs creaked as we followed the man, cups and jackets in our hands. There was a shaft of light entering the room from the right side of the lake. The upstairs smelled of pine. He left a little brazier on the table for us. The embers inside were glowing.

Her hands as she placed them on top of the brazier were as beautiful as her face. And very young. She moved a bit. The shaft of light lit up her face.

'Chef Kirpal,' she said, 'Irem never told me this. She never said a word about that incident you describe.'

Then we were silent.

I don't know from where the courage came but then I reached out and touched Rubiya's cheek. She did not turn her face.

'I feel relieved talking to you, Rubiya,' I said.

She did not say anything.

'Why are you so silent?'

'Chef Kirpal,' she asked, 'why is this world such a disappointing place?'

I was at a loss for words.

'Chef,' she almost hit me, 'I am angry at Father. Very angry. I am angry he did this, and I am sad he is dead. But I am also very angry that he is dead.'

'I am sorry,' I said. 'Perhaps I should not have — '

'You did nothing wrong. But.'

'But what?'

'Now I must leave,' she said. 'The bus leaves at five in the afternoon.'

'Please do not go.'

'I must.'

'In that case I must tell you for one last time how much your poems mean to me.'

'Chef Kirpal, poetry makes not a thing happen.'

'No. Rubiya. No. Your poems have changed me. I feel like running through the streets, through the narrow trails, I feel like climbing up the mountains to request the people of Kashmir not to lose compassion for us Indians, and I feel like telling my own countrymen not to lose compassion for Kashmiris. Rubiya, your words are helping people like me to say things we want to say.'

'Chef Kirpal, are you all right?'

Outside it had temporarily stopped snowing. The roofs of houses covered with layers looked beautiful. Black-and-white smoke arose from the chimneys. The boats in the lake were absolutely motionless. The chenar trees, on both sides of the road, were heavy with snow. The sky above them was filled with clouds and absolutely red. The road was white, but the sky was red. Two horsemen passed by.

'I will accompany you to the bus terminal.'

'No, please don't. It is easier this way.'

She removed her jacket from the peg.

'Chef Kirpal, from this window at exactly five o'clock you will be able to see the bus to Pakistan. Just stay here. This is the perfect place to say farewell to me. I will wave at you from the bus.'

'OK. I will stay.'

'Chef Kirpal, I sense you are sick. Your eyes blink as if you are about to collapse.'

'Please do not worry. Nothing wrong with me.'

'Before I leave, Chef Kirpal, tell me about yourself. Tell me what you felt towards Irem.'

'I do not know.'

For some unknown reason at that moment I thought about my mother. The way she used to spend so many hours in the kitchen, never eating with those at the table, always serving. Cooking was her way to say how she felt towards people close to her.

'I do not know,' I said to Rubiya, 'I do not

327

know how I felt towards Irem, but now that I think of it, now that you have asked me, I think that that feeling must have been special.'

In the brazier the embers were dying fast, and Rubiya hugged me, and then she left. She walked out of the door, I heard her steps on the wooden stairs, and I slowly sat down in the chair by the window, and started my second cup of tea, and dunked bakerkhani, the fragile Kashmiri pastry, in tea, and all of a sudden the past started coming back to me, and I felt as if I was soaking up vast expanses of time, and I recalled that long ago day when I had visited Irem in the hospital and the first thing she had said after a long silence, You smell of garlic. What can I do? I had asked. Garlic has entered the pores of my skin. Try a lemon, she had said. It always works.

It has not worked, I almost say to her.

Irem, I almost say.

At five I stood up, and saw the bus to Pakistan pass by the tea house, and slowly, as I waved, the vehicle became a fuzzy vapor, indistinguishable from the road. Somewhere inside my brain I heard a vibration, the Ninth, coming to a close. Several times my hand tried to reach out for her, but her bus kept moving further and further, receding into that forbidden land, until it became a little black dot. I felt it was time to rest for a while, because there was still a lot more work to do, a lot more cooking. Then it began to snow.

Acknowledgements

I am grateful to the Canada Council for the Arts, the Corporation of Yaddo, the Markin-Flanagan Distinguished Writers' Program, le Conseil des Arts et des Lettres du Québec, and the Banff Centre for the Arts for providing assistance to create this work.

The poem 'Afterwards' appeared originally in *danDelion* (vol. 33, #1). Irem is modeled partially on Shahnaz Kauser, someone I read about in newspaper articles by Mannika Chopra: 'A Pakistani Mother Speaks of Life in Indian Jail Limbo' (*The Boston Globe*, June 2002) and Khalid Hasan: 'Jailed in India, Unwanted in Pakistan' (*Friday Times*, August 2002). 'Had Saadat Hasan Manto been alive, he would have written a story about Shahnaz Kauser.' This one line moved and inspired me throughout the creation of this work. Shahnaz's story has been best told in Sumantra Bose's *Kashmir: Roots of Conflict, Paths to Peace* (Harvard University Press, 2005). Thanks to Pankaj Mishra (*New York Review of Books*) and Basharat Peer (*Curfewed Night*) for bold reporting on Kashmir that brought attention to 'interrogation camps' like Papa-1 and Papa-2. I relied on several publications to understand Siachen or Rose Glacier, starting with the 1912 expedition accounts of Fanny Bullock Workman. No one has written better on Siachen than Amitav Ghosh in *Countdown* (Ravi Dayal, 1999) and Kevin Fedarko, 'The Coldest War' (*Outsider*, February 2003). I am indebted to both for valuable information. Other books I found useful include: *Conflict Without End* (Viking, 2002) by Lt. Gen. (Retd.) V. R. Raghavan, *War at the Top of the World* (Key Porter, 1999) by Eric Margolis, and *Behind the Vale* (Roli, 2003) by M. J. Akbar. Thanks to the outspoken Indian army soldiers and officers for sharing Kashmir stories. Every flake of snow (and if I may, every glacier) begins with a nucleation site, a tiny particle. That tiny particle (for this book) was my inability to comprehend the early death of the poet Agha Shahid Ali (1949–2001). These pages are immensely inspired by his life and work.

I would like to thank everyone at Véhicule Press (Montreal), especially Nancy Marrelli, Bruce Henry and Simon Dardick. To Bloomsbury, and Penguin India. For their generous advice on early drafts thanks to

Umarraj Singh Saberwal, Chef Olivier Fuldauer, Renuka Chatterjee, Robert Majzels, Lissa Cowan, and Nidhi Srinivas. Thanks (for many reasons) to Adi, Rosa, Amit Pal, Janice Lee, Dilreen Kaur, Farhat Rehman, Denise Drury, Agatha Schwartz, Aparna Sundar and Taras Grescoe. To Chef Cameron Stauch, whom I interviewed in New Delhi, to Jerome Lowenthal, my 'Beethoven consultant', to Lorna Crozier (the line in italics on page 128 is inspired by her poetry collection *The Sex Lives of Vegetables*), to Maria José de la Macorra for the sketch on page 42, to Negar Akhavi for sharing the Dalai Lama 'Chinese gulag' story, to Nadia Kurd, Riaz Mehmood and Wajahat Ahmad for the Kashmiri translation and Perso-Arabic script on page 172.

Special thanks to Andrew Steinmetz, Jackie Kaiser, Natasha Daneman and Alexandra Pringle.

We do hope that you have enjoyed reading
this large print book.

Did you know that all of our titles
are available for purchase?

We publish a wide range of high quality
large print books including:
Romances, Mysteries, Classics
General Fiction
Non Fiction and Westerns

Special interest titles available in
large print are:
The Little Oxford Dictionary
Music Book
Song Book
Hymn Book
Service Book

Also available from us courtesy of
Oxford University Press:
Young Readers' Dictionary
(large print edition)
Young Readers' Thesaurus
(large print edition)

For further information or a free
brochure, please contact us at:
Ulverscroft Large Print Books Ltd.,
The Green, Bradgate Road, Anstey,
Leicester, LE7 7FU, England.
Tel: (00 44) 0116 236 4325
Fax: (00 44) 0116 234 0205

Other titles published by
The House of Ulverscroft:

MATHILDA SAVITCH

Victor Lodato

Fear doesn't come naturally to Mathilda Savitch. She looks directly at things that others cannot bring themselves to mention: for example, the fact that her beloved sister is dead; pushed in front of a train by a man still at large. Her grief-stricken parents have been basically sleepwalking ever since, and Mathilda is going to shock them back to life. Her strategy? Being bad. She decides to investigate the catastrophe, sleuthing through her sister's secret possessions — anything she can ferret out. But Mathilda risks a great deal — she must leave behind everything she loves in order to discover the truth.

AN UNFINISHED BUSINESS

Boualem Sansal

Rachel and Malrich Schiller, sons of a German father and an Algerian mother, are educated in Paris. Rachel excels and works for a multinational, but Malrich grows up in the banlieues and mixes with the wrong crowd. When their parents are killed in an Islamic fundamentalist raid, Rachel soon discovers that his father, a reputed chemist before the war, joined the Nazi party and then the SS. He finds the attempt to trace his true heritage and confront the Holocaust, one of the great taboos of Muslim culture, unbearable. It's left to the streetwise Malrich to complete the unfinished business.

OUT OF THE STORM

Janet Thomas

It's 1901. In a sleepy Cornish fishing village, whilst one woman struggles with an agonising choice, another suffers endless brutality: Kate seizes the opportunity to break out of her trap with both hands, but can she turn her experiences into something positive? Loveday is desperate for a baby of her own, but will she find joy or heartbreak along the way? Here, then, are two sisters, two secrets. Two women who have the courage to turn their lives around, but can they live with the consequences?